THE

BLAKE
HETHERINGTON

MYSTERIES

D S NELSON

To David
fellow author
D S Nelson

Black Hat Books

THE BLAKE HETHERINGTON MYSTERIES

First published 2014 by Black Hat Books

ISBN: 978-0-9928480-0-2

Copyright © D S Nelson 2014

www.dsnelson.co.uk

info@dsnelson.co.uk

Cover art based on original artwork by Nancy Thompson and adapted by A Bit Wordy.

CONTENTS

HATS OFF TO MURDER

BLAKE HETHERINGTON MYSTERY #1

The Bowler

'Henry Bollinger of Kensington and formerly Epsom, Surrey, passed away on Tuesday, 11th September 2012, aged 52 years. Son of the late Michael and Sarah Bollinger. Much loved brother of Susan and brother-in-law to John. Funeral service at Christ Church, Epsom Common, on Wednesday, September 26th, at 11.00am, followed by interment.'

Reading the obituaries, whilst drinking my ten o' clock coffee, is a habit I developed upon reaching my sixtieth birthday; I've found age makes one a little morbid. It was during the month of September that I discovered a couple of my *'regular'* customers had unfortunately met their end. Henry Bollinger was a regular customer and although his ending seemed at first innocuous, as with all things in life, if you want the full story you must look a little closer.

In the hat trade a regular customer is one that visits your establishment perhaps once a year. Hat repairs, fickle fashions and adornments can sometimes mean more frequent visits, up to say three times a year, but I pride myself on the quality of my stock; repairs simply do not feature that often. Perhaps a nasty incident with a coat hook or a misplaced hat on a seat with a rear bearing down upon it might warrant such a visit, but never a lack of workmanship.

I am the fifth Hetherington to own a hat shop. Some say hats were the first item of clothing worn by humans. I'm not so sure myself, a chap has to have the right outfit to go with the hat, but say we suspend our disbelief for a second and decide hats are indeed the oldest apparel to adorn the human race. That would make hat making the oldest profession on earth.

When I am not serving customers or reading the paper, I watch the street outside the shop. The view from my window affords me ample fodder for one of my favourite pastimes: people watching. Of course there is also a professional advantage to this hobby. A milliner must understand his client, capture their personality and crown them with it. Although I may only speak to them for a couple of hours a year, knowing my customer well is still important to me. My longstanding experience and careful observation allows me to gather information about a customer based on their hat purchases. I can glean a lot from a snatched conversation. In order to perfect this skill however, I must also know my hats.

Of course there are other clues. For example the olfactory nature of London makes for some interesting assumptions about a person. Sometimes a hat has a certain smell about it. The whiff of smoke from an open fire, expensive perfume, hair wax or mothballs. The odd adornment also provides a window into the mind-set of its wearer and the turn of the brim allows a person to control the outsiders' view. The fact remains, however, that when a hat begins life there is little to give away its future; once it is possessed it becomes a map of its owner.

Following Thursday's obituary, a small column in Friday's paper piqued my interest by alerting me to Henry Bollinger's true fate. Some holidaymakers discovered his body whilst trying to negotiate a lock. He was face down, floating in the canal - caught up against the sluice (to my distress there was no mention of his trademark bowler, ruined no doubt). The inquest's verdict was a heart attack. The fact that Mr Bollinger happened to have been walking near the lock at the time of the event was an unfortunate coincidence. So why am I interested in the death of Henry Bollinger and what is the significance of his attire?

First we must start with the bowler hat. What could be more English than the silhouette of a bowler hat? Originally designed in the 1850s for game wardens as a sort of hardhat, the bowler has, through the ages, adorned the heads of many as a symbol of both power and solidarity. It can mean many things; you could be anyone under a bowler - who knows whose side you're on. A peasant woman from Peru or worse, a banker!

Henry Bollinger was one such customer. A typical bowler: plutocratic and proud, yet difficult to judge. There were some facts I gleaned from our conversations: for example he worked in a bank and was a devout bachelor. He had a red-faced indignant look about him. A slight lisp suggested that at some point in his well-educated life he might have required elocution lessons. His hat gave away the faint smell of Cuban tobacco and money. It can be assumed that for Henry Bollinger, on returning home from work, a cigar was habitual.

When he spoke his voice was nasal and sharp and yet his conversation was jovial and pleasant creating a dichotomy of image. The only giveaway of Henry Bollinger's true nature was the feather tucked into the hatband of his bowler: a bright red and perfectly preened little feather. It was a special order as the feather of a Scarlet Ibis is hard to come by, nevertheless forty years in the hat trade means that I have my contacts.

I'm a great believer in the symbolism of colour. Colour sets the personality for many a hat. Red has many meanings from danger to love; but all are associated with man's most basic urges. He may simply have been a fly fisherman and this was a symbol of his hobby he liked to keep close. It is a mystery to me indeed, that such a man should meet his end at Camden Locks; it's hardly a dignified place to die.

Why? You may well ask. A heart attack ending in a dip in the canal is a perfectly legitimate means of meeting one's maker, but to me it just didn't sit right. The first problem with this unfortunate death was the smell. The canal in the summer has a very distinct aroma. Even the most expensive perfumes cannot hide the faint stagnant smell that remains on your clothing if you have been walking in this area. Henry Bollinger's clothing never had the odour of canal about it. Cigars yes, money definitely but canals no.

The second anomaly was that the late Mr Bollinger did not seem the sort to walk home. He was a Kensington man and it is well known that men of Kensington take taxis. On top of that, he did not strike me as the sort to loiter around the canal long enough to fall in.

The third and final overwhelming fact was the banker wore a bowler! You can be anyone under a bowler. So do you see my problem? These facts led me to wonder whom the real Henry Bollinger was and what was he doing at Camden Locks?

The Stetson

'American millionaire Hank Cartwright tragically died in a riding accident yesterday. One of London's high profile socialites, Mr Cartwright leaves behind him a wife and two children. In a statement to the press his wife said "He loved his horses and if Hank had a choice in how he was going to go, this would have been it". She goes on to describe him as a loving man who had time for everyone.

Mrs Cartwright intends to return to America where she can be near her family at this difficult time. She extends her gratitude to the people of London for the flowers and tributes she has already received. She hopes to return in the New Year to arrange the sale of their London home on Cornwall Terrace, Regents Park. The property is expected to reach in excess of £35 million. Mr Cartwright's eldest son is set to inherit the American-based ranches.'

It was almost two weeks later when I noticed the article regarding the demise of Hank Cartwright. As a prolific hat buyer, he was a customer I was unlikely to forget and his death made a not insignificant dent in my turnover. Hats are a serious business to an American ranch-owner, especially one who owns six ranches and several racehorses.

So why was I interested in the misfortunes of an American millionaire? Well, apart from the aforementioned dip in profits there are some things about Hank Cartwright's death that don't quite add up. But first let me tell you a little about our American.

His choice of hat was, of course, the Stetson. The Stetson represents attitude; a deep-rooted culture of taciturn and plain weary cowboys who work hard for their livings and spit on their shoes to polish them. To me, the Stetson is indeed representative of ambivalent men who use few words, unless of course we are talking about Hank Cartwright.

With the insistence that I called him Hank and not Mr Cartwright, his visits were more like a friend popping in to discuss the weather and the affairs of the day. If the man were not such a gentleman, I might be given to describing his conversations as a little akin to verbal diarrhoea. This did not mean, however, that I knew any more about him than some of my less regular customers. It is the quality of information that leads to accurate deductions, not the quantity.

Some say the customisation of the Stetson indicates the importance of a person, a little like the height of a chef's Toque Blanche but to Hank Cartwright this did not apply. Despite his millionaire status, for Hank the Stetson for him, was a plain and simple version. The only thing it had to be was new. No feathers, badges, toggles or rope, just a plain and elegant Stetson. His only concession to fashion was a Carlsbad crease that sloped forward allowing him to take a firm grip of the hat in order to tip the brim and shade his eyes from the world.

He was always well turned out: typically, blue jeans and a shirt with a bolo tie. His swarthy weather-beaten skin was pocked-marked, indicative of childhood acne. More often than not he smelt strongly of stables and horses, an oddly comforting smell, but there was no tell-tale strand of straw in his treads or mud on his turn-ups.

You would expect him, as a man of means in his late fifties, to have retired and left the hard work to his sons;

but for Hank to be parted from his beloved horses would surely have been purgatory. As a result, he still frequently returned to America to attend to business.

Hank was what you might think of as a stereotypical American ranch-owner, but he often surprised me. His love of the arts and history translated into a somewhat encyclopaedic knowledge of the master painters of Europe. He would often admire the picture of the Duchess of Devonshire by Thomas Gainsborough that I have hanging in the shop (a copy of course; but he was too much a gentleman to mention it).

But what had any of this got to do with his death, I hear you ask, and why did I think there were any malevolent forces at work? He did indeed die as a result of a riding accident. Broke his neck according to the coroner. A rather violent but mercifully quick death I should think. The article in the paper goes on to say that his horse was spooked by the sound of gunshot from a nearby pheasant shoot. It is here I encountered the first conundrum.

To my knowledge the pheasant season doesn't start until the first week in October. Granted, perhaps they were shooting grouse or pigeons, but I think not. You see Hank Cartwright was on his own land when he died. I know from our conversations that he only kept pheasants for the shooting season and his land is private, only being rented out for organised shoots. So what was someone doing shooting on his land out of season? If I am incorrect about it being the wrong season and they were actually shooting pheasants, why was Mr Cartwright out riding when there was a shoot nearby, organised presumably by himself?

The next problem I have rather goes hand in hand with the first problem. As I have explained, Hank Cartwright was the owner of several large ranches and, therefore, was a very experienced horseman. As a ranch-owner used to stampeding cattle and bucking horses, how on earth did he lose control of his most favoured steed? This again suggests to me that the gunshot heard was far from expected. Had there been an organised shoot he would surely he would have refrained from riding that day.

Finally, and not without significance, is the reaction of his wife to his demise. I have no doubt the lady is distraught, however, I was given to understand that her sons were residing in London and that she did not exactly see eye-to-eye with her mother who remained in America. So why then would she return so quickly to the bosom of her American family?

It is an arguable fact that a death in a family does bring people together and heal old rifts but I still fail to see why she would leave her sons who, by all accounts, are most supportive. They will obviously have to return to America themselves at some point to settle the matter of the ranches, but, Mr Cartwright informed me that his sons had married women, rooted firmly in England, and that he was the proud grandfather of five. I hardly think her daughters-in-law will relish the thought of moving their young families to America and, in the process, move further away from their own families.

None of it made sense at all and I couldn't help but wonder if the genial Hank Cartwright hadn't met with more than an accident.

The Fedora

It is at this juncture I think it apt to tell you about a very interesting customer of mine named Antony Gargano. He has not frequented my shop for some months now, although I am inclined to believe he has returned to Italy rather than met with an unfortunate demise. His last visit was on one of the last days in September and there was something about it that made it stand out amongst the more mundane.

Signor Gargano is quite a tall man, for an Italian; his dark blonde hair and blue-grey eyes enhance his atypical appearance. Despite this he has the tanned skin of a Sicilian and his Fedora announces his heritage to the world.

Of course, the Fedora is an adaptation of the Trilby often worn by the dapper smooth talking crook, perhaps associated more with your Bugsy Malone types. Myself, I don't believe in that particular myth. For example the Bloomsbury Set, a distinctly unfelonious group of intellectuals, wore Trilbies and Fedoras. Therefore, the romance of the Fedora can create an interesting disunion between hat and hat owner, for Fedoras, like Bowlers, can be owned by a variety of different people with very different motives - some not all that romantic.

The strong smell of aftershave mingled with the aroma of home cooking, suggested that, at the time, he had a good woman to look after him. His choice of pinstripe suits and his impeccable English led me to the entirely assumed conclusion that, although Italian by nature, his nurture had in fact occurred on this fair isle.

From our conversations, I gleaned his love of the Tate, opera, and walks along the South Bank. His mannerisms were carefully crafted and deliberate. But for the more astute observer there was a tiny window into his soul – the humming.

When deep in thought, perhaps examining a potential new purchase, he would hum quietly to himself, always the same tune. Verdi's Rigoletto I believe: '*La donna è mobile, qual piuma al vento, muta d'accento, e di pensiero.¹*', I can hear him humming it now.

Signor Gargano first caught my interest when he mentioned an art gallery, which I had not heard of before. This in itself was not particularly unusual. Please be assured that I do not have the pretensions to think that I have heard of every worthwhile establishment in the city. London is a sprawling metropolis of culture and every day a new venture appears, casting its hat into the ring, as it were. What was unusual was the location of the gallery. The Limehouse Basin was not somewhere I associated with the fine arts, more a community of industry where you may be more likely to find heavy machinery than delicate brushstrokes.

He reported to me that one Flora Delibes owned the gallery. A somewhat demure name to be found in the Limehouse Basin, I'm sure. He described it as a small gallery with only the finest art housed within and urged me to visit, indicating the Gainsborough as he did and perhaps assuming it was not the fake I knew it to be.

He owned several pieces himself, which I understood to be mainly by Italian artists and although he never mentioned whom, he had led me to believe they were fine examples of their time. This confused me as I imagined a man with his keen interest in art must surely know a counterfeit Gainsborough when he sees one; especially one so inexpertly executed. Perhaps he too, like Cartwright, was too much of a gentleman to comment.

All of this brings me to the last visit Gargano made to the shop towards the end of August. It was then that Bowler and Fedora met.

Bank holiday weekends often make for particularly busy days in the shop as last minute hat repairs or purchases are required for garden parties, days at the races and other such social engagements. My customers do not usually socialise on account of it being a) in London and b) not a café. It is entered for one purpose and one purpose only - to buy a hat. I have resisted several salesmen's attempts to sell me coffee machines for my establishment. My position on this matter: new hats and hot drinks do not mix well.

This event stands out however because Mr Bollinger and Signor Gargano acknowledged each other. You may say this is not entirely abnormal: a busy shop, a sunny day, we are all human; perhaps the need to acknowledge one another's existence isn't that rare. I repeat, however, that this is London. One does not acknowledge people one doesn't know in such a big city, as one cannot be sure whom one is acknowledging.

During the brief conversation that ensued between the two, I saw Signor Gargano's face redden as he rubbed the back of his neck. A tug of his tie and a straightening of his jacket suggested a level of discomfort, which I had never before seen in Gargano. In contrast Henry Bollinger observed Gargano's discomfort with a cock of his head and confident grin.

So what? The slight nod of a head, a brief conversation conducted through the corners of mouths it could be anything. Bollinger, however, was a lover of money, a banker and financier, Gargano a lover of art and culture. In my experience the two do not often meet as friends, unless of course the latter has money in which the former would be interested. Perhaps this was the case that day, but when a Bowler and a Fedora meet, one can never be too sure of the reasoning; two hats, stereotypical in nature, and yet easily capable of misleading the casual observer.

Indeed what was real and what was false about Antony Gargano? He had knowledge of, at least 'popular', opera (the humming proved as much) but did he really have an appreciation of art or was this a deliberate screen behind which he hid a less cultured past?

The greatest puzzle to me was that if he was indeed the considered and seemingly sophisticated man he appeared to be, then why would he have anything to do with the pompous peacock that was Bollinger, let alone defer to him? To all intents and purposes there seemed to be only one answer - Bollinger had some kind of hold over Gargano.

---

[1] *Woman is flighty, like a feather in the wind; she changes in voice and in thought.*

The Hatinator

I did not attend the aforementioned Limehouse Basin gallery until a month or so later and not at the behest of Signor Gargano. It was instead for another far more intriguing proposition, which I will now impart.

It was October when I heard again of Flora Delibes. It was on one of those autumnal mornings when the wind is strong enough to warrant two hatpins. A young lady entered my shop in a flurry of leaves. Despite the hurly burly outside, she had managed to retain a fascinator and it was not from my shop! I do, of course, sell fascinators but I did not sell this one.

Essentially an oversized hair decoration, over the last few years, to my alarm, fascinators have increased in size until they are now frequently referred to as *'hatinators'* (although I am loathed to use the phrase).

Some very well respected designers have recently crafted, among their commissions, some formidable *'hatinators'*. Their purpose to me is unclear, neither a hat nor a fascinator. Perhaps they are designed to detract from the wearers face; I really wouldn't like to comment further.

Whilst the wearers may think themselves chic and modern, we are in fact dealing with a good old pillbox hat. Pierre Cardin may have rocked the 1960's with his elaborate and frankly impractical creations, leading to the later work of Treacy and Jones, but in the end we always return faithfully to tradition.

This piece was definitely a *'hatinator'*; a bright red heart shaped pillbox sitting proudly on her hairline with a carefully crafted lock of hair flirtatiously curling up to meet it. Vulgar white cording exaggerated the shape giving what you might call a high definition effect to the creation. The gaudy red mesh that adorned it served no function other than to accentuate the monstrous nature of the apparition before me. There was nothing sophisticated about this hat and yet I was transfixed.

The lady herself was pretty and well mannered. Her soft brown curls framed her face in a neat bob and the wind chill had given a glow to her cheeks that was wholesome and natural. Biting her lip, she approached the counter, offered me a well-manicured hand and introduced herself as '...*the daughter of gallery owner Flora Delibes: Delilah*'. Her nature did not match that of her hat. I gave her a smile that I have perfected over the years: just the right amount of welcome and professionalism, without appearing patronising or condescending. It seemed to work for what occurred next can only be described as a tsunami of words: not something I am used to receiving.

The speed at which she spoke was breath taking, punctuated only by the occasional animated eyebrow. As she spoke she leant forward on the counter towards me and the scent of Chanel No.5 tickled my nose. I watched as her lips enunciated each word. It is fair to say that, had I been several decades younger, I may well have taken a shine to Miss Delibes. On finishing she took a step back, straightened and awaited my reply. So fascinated by the hatinator was I that I had not noticed until this point the Jack Russell that sat obediently by her Christian Lacroix clad feet. It too looked up at me expectantly.

It appeared Miss Delibes' mother had gone missing. Unable to approach the police and fearing the worst, she had come to me. '*Why?*' you may well ask, as did I. It transpires that Miss Delibes was engaged to a Jay Cartwright, the youngest of the Cartwright sons. A son I was not aware of, as Mr Cartwright had only ever spoken of two sons, Devon and Owen, but to my memory never Jay. This in itself intrigued me, but I digress.

According to Miss Delibes, Mr Cartwright Senior had spoken of me on several occasions. He had gone so far as to say that should she ever be in need of help then Mr Blake Hetherington of Hetherington's Hats, was her man. I suggested that perhaps he had been referring to matters of fashion, eying her headwear. However she was most insistent that he in fact referred to my measured nature and my understanding of the psychology of the human mind. Flattered, I was hardly going to contradict the lady.

During a further exchange I came to understand that Ms Flora Delibes had been missing for almost three weeks. Delilah had at first not thought this unusual as, after the failure of Flora Delibes' third marriage, she would often disappear on a cruise for up to four weeks at a time. However, Miss Delibes usually received a postcard at some point during these absences, something she had not received this time.

Miss Delibes still shared a home with her mother and her concern had reached its zenith when an Italian named Gargano, closely followed by a French woman named Derenne, called at the house enquiring after her mother and why the gallery was not open for business. On this point, and this point only, I raised my eyebrows.

When I again reiterated that I was unsure as to what help I could possibly be and that surely informing the police would be a far more appropriate course of action she started to pace the shop floor, the little dog shadowing her every move. She was at pains to explain that she could under no circumstances go to the police but she did not explain why. She felt her fiancé was too preoccupied with the death of his father to worry about the disappearance of a mother-in-law he did not like. She followed this with an appeal to my good nature and character as a gentleman. Well, how could I refuse?

By the time she left, I was a little unsure as to how the events had come to pass. My memory was a haze of sweet-smelling perfume and the urgent supplication of a gaudy pillbox '*hatinator*.'

I was to meet her later that evening at a barge named, The Rattenbury, moored on the Regent's Canal, not far from the Wentlock Arms. There I would meet her fiancé, Mr Jay Cartwright and she would take me to the infamous gallery of Flora Delibes.

Once again, I was left with more questions than answers. Why Hank Cartwright had thought it necessary to mention me to Delilah is still a mystery to me even as I tell you this story. My only conclusion is that he saw something in me that I thought I'd kept hidden (I like to observe, I do not wish to be observed). Despite this, a duty had fallen upon me to help Miss Delibes in her hour of need and I hoped not to fail her.

The Gainsborough

When I arrived at the The Rattenbury later that evening, Miss Delibes was waiting on the towpath, thankfully minus the hatinator. The cold breeze heralded the inevitability of the impending winter and we had both pulled our coats tight as we walked.

Jay Cartwright was not to join us that evening as he had a prior engagement, of which Miss Delibes had not been aware. She apologised and suggested that before visiting the gallery we should go for dinner, at her expense, so she could apprise me of the various facts. Her choice was a gastro-pub named 'The Snicket'. One of the older buildings situated alongside the basin, it has a charming aspect with excellent views of the river.

I sampled my starter of herb-crusted scallops and Miss Delibes began her tale. It was evident that her mother's two great loves were art and her only daughter, but I was sure there was far more to this woman than these facts alone and I waited patiently for it to be revealed.

Lo and behold, about a week before her mother had disappeared, Delilah had become aware of an affair Ms Delibes was conducting. Having never met her mother's admirer, the only information she had was that the man was originally from Sicily and that they had met at the opera. Delilah concluded, taking into account his recent visit that the man must be Gargano.

The attentive service did not seem to stall Miss Delibes, although her spiced butternut squash soup remained untouched for some time. The smells emanating from the kitchen had me longing for the second course, despite my interest in Miss Delibes' story.

More wine was poured as the sea bream and duck appeared for the main course so I took advantage of the lull in Miss Delibes' monologue and ignored the grumblings of my stomach. I mentioned that Mr Gargano was one of my clients and seemed a happily married man who spent a fair amount of his time in Sicily. I confirmed that I too had the suspicion that he was the same Gargano connected to her mother in some way especially given the reference to opera. She was surprised and pressed me for more information.

I bought up the subject of the painting in my establishment, its doubtful provenance and how Mr Gargano's interest in it perplexed me. Dabbing her mouth with her napkin, she had blushed and lowered her eyes. As I tucked into my bream, she pushed almost untouched duck to one side and at last told me of the true nature of her mother's gallery and possibly the reason for Mr Gargano's interest.

It was a front; the art was fake, as far as she knew, although she wasn't supposed to. Her mother would not have wanted her daughter to know and, she assumed, did not want to jeopardise Flora's chances of marrying into one of the most affluent families in the city. Hence she could not report her mother's absence to the police for fear of drawing unwanted attention to the gallery. She had come to me in the hope that I may be discreet. Finishing my main course, my appetite, for the moment, satiated, I chose to broach the subject of her fiancé,

'And your affianced, I trust, is still ignorant of this fact?' I had asked

Miss Delibes nodded affirmation. It was at this point I wondered if Miss Delibes' intention had ever really been for us to dine with Mr Cartwright. Surely, for him to accompany us would have meant for him to be a party to this conversation. A conversation I assumed Miss Delibes did not to want to have with Jay Cartwright. A unnecessary obscuring of facts, or deliberate attempt to mislead me, as to Mr Cartwright's involvement in this subterfuge?

Dessert was lemon posset. Miss Delibes abstained, choosing instead an Amaretto liqueur. She hunched her shoulders, cupped the glass close and at my request, with a contented smile, began to tell me about the mysterious Jay Cartwright.

Miss Delibes met Jay whilst working behind the bar of the Wentlock Arms during her university days. Despite appearances, her mother had not been able to finance her Cambridge education and so the canal-side pub had been a means of supporting herself during the summer.

The youngest Cartwright's dark hair and Dallas accent had melted her heart. She had fallen for him hook line and sinker. Jay earned his living as a shipbroker and they were saving for the big white wedding they both wanted. Whilst they saved Miss Delibes was still living with her mother, primarily because The Rattenbury did not hold the comfort she was used to.

Miss Delibes had been engaged to Jay Cartwright since graduating from Cambridge, four years ago. She had obtained a Master in Archaeology specialising in European prehistory. I was impressed. After a couple of years voluntary work and the good fortune to receive some recent lottery funding, Miss Delibes had secured herself a job as a field archaeologist and thankfully had no need of bar work these days. I found it hard to imagine the young lady in front of me up to her elbows in mud eulogising about Roman artefacts, but nevertheless there was definitely more to Miss Delibes than a terrible taste in hats.

Miss Delibes went on to reveal that Jay had never been close to his father. They had fallen out over a teenage prank, which had gone wrong and led to both a criminal record and a stint in juvenile correction centre. He became the proverbial black sheep and rarely had anything to do with the rest of his family. Despite Mr Cartwright's disagreement with his son, he had left him a small sum of money in his will, which would allow him to marry Delilah the next year and hopefully buy a house.

Our visit to the gallery was by now long overdue. Miss Delibes insisted on settling the bill and refused to take any remuneration from myself, we then proceeded along the canal.

The Limehouse Gallery had been established in 2010 when Flora Delibes had received an inheritance from her brother. Built on the corner of Basin Approach, the gallery naturally had a mooring. I noted that a small yacht; named *Bel Fiore* was attached to this mooring. Miss Delibes had made no mention of a passion for sailing, yet she had mentioned nearly everything else, so I made a mental note to ask her about it later.

It was a functional brick building that housed the artwork. The glass frontage allowed a handsome view of the canal. The only thing that reminded one of the proximity of the city was the Docklands Light Railway rumbling by above.

Towards the back of the gallery was a small mahogany desk and Miss Delibes directed me towards it. She suggested I look through the papers, which covered the top of the desk, and also in the drawers, to see if there was anything that might indicate the whereabouts of her mother. Still a little unsure as to why she thought I would be any more able than she, I attempted to protest, citing my limited knowledge of art, but she insisted and I began to sort through the paperwork. The lady had bought me dinner, after all.

The desk was littered with what appeared at first glance to be invoices, letters and receipts. Most of these were fairly standard business transactions however ill-filed and the names Gargano and Derenne appeared several times, I have to say, this was not to my surprise.

In the top drawer of the desk was an appointment book. Under the appointment book was a picture of a very handsome woman and written on the back was - *All my love T - Summer 2009'.* Miss Delibes enlightened me of the fact that I was looking at the owner of the gallery. Delilah was able to tell me the picture had been taken on one of her mother's trips but not who *T* was. Extrapolating the *T* from Tony, as in 'Antony', I assumed this to be Mr Gargano's handwriting.

Sat Hepburn-esque on a picnicking rug, Flora Delibes was giving the photographer a coy smile. A fine looking Gainsborough hat shaded her face from the sun and if the picture had not been dated you may have been forgiven for thinking she was from another era.

I was cheered by the presence of such a hat. Celebrities will often try sunglasses but I think hats are a much more effective distraction technique, particularly the Gainsborough, and it appeared Flora Delibes was of the same mind. However, the hat can attract too much attention, and in fact have quite the opposite effect. In Flora Delibes case it gave the unfortunate impression of a lady whom, as the late Mr Cartwright might say, is *'all hat and no cattle'.*

In the second drawer were some more revealing documents, letters discussing the requirements of various customers with photographs of the paintings attached. Miss Delibes had obviously left in a hurry, because these somewhat incriminating letters remained in an unlocked drawer for anyone to stumble upon.

It had been a long day, it was getting late and Miss Delibes was anxious to return home to her little dog. With Miss Delibes consent, I took the invoices, appointment book and photograph away with me to study at a later date. Curiosity had got the better of me and the Delibes had my attention. I had to know how a woman, with such a flamboyant hat, could simply disappear.

The Beret

As fortune would have it, it was not long before the next piece of the jigsaw puzzle revealed itself.

It came, of course, in the form of Miss Derenne, a visit I did not anticipate. Up until this point she had been a shadowy figure, inhabiting the corners of my imagination. The personification, however, did not reveal a great deal more.

Exactly one week after my dinner with Miss Delibes, the usual midweek lull in custom had afforded me the time to finally peruse some of the invoices and accounts I had acquired on my visit to the Limehouse Basin gallery. I was completely immersed in my task. There seemed to have been plenty of business conducted with the aforementioned Derenne and of course Gargano. This led me to believe they may be in cahoots with Ms Flora Delibes and I was eager to find definitive evidence.

You can imagine I was all astonishment, when a petite and very French lady approached the shop counter, interrupting my studies. She was wearing an oversized crimson-red beret, which coupled with her transient glances, implied a surreptitious nature. She toyed with me initially, complimenting me on the excellence of my merchandise and bemoaning the loss of quality handmade products in today's consumer society. I nodded and 'mm'd' in the appropriate places until her eyes finally set on my hairline and she came to her point,

'Do you know Monsieur Cartwright?'

Thinking myself clever, I of course replied, 'Which one?'

At that point she chose to make eye contact, immersing me in a gaze that would have had the Saints confessing. Her green eyes were like Amazonian plunge pools and for a moment or two I was lost.

'Monsieur 'ank Cartwright?' She replied, smiling.

Dragging myself away from her eyes and focussing instead on the ridiculous beret, I gathered my thoughts. As I did so, I chose to think on that hat.

Irrevocably associated with left wing politics and spies, the beret is not a hat to hide under. Even more so when wearing an oversized one, as the wearer runs the risk of appearing as if they were a little girl who has raided their mother's wardrobe for dressing up attire. The Frenchness of this character was too ridiculous for words and she lacked the class I expected - and that Miss Delibes had described - but this had to be Miss Derenne.

My next question therefore should perhaps have been my first, but I was caught up in assumptions and that enormous beret,

'Who, may I ask, are you?'

With the skill of a magician, she produced a business card from her gloved hand, placed it on the counter and tapped at the name printed on it in elaborate cursive text. This was indeed, Mademoiselle Derenne, an arts and antiques dealer from gay Paris.

'Je suis un marchande d'art à Paris', she smiled again. It was a benign smile designed to placate. 'Je pensais que vous connais peut- être Monsieur Cartwright'.

Was perhaps her use of French was an attempt at flattery? Did she mean me to think she was not as competent at English as she had first shown? Perhaps she intended me to reply in French so we may speak without being overheard, but the shop was empty. Smoke and mirrors are always an interesting diversion, but smoke stings the eyes and I never like to see my own reflection, so I did not reply in French.

'And what would lead Mademoiselle to me?' Was my next, more deliberate, question.

Her reply, in English this time, impressed me more than I care to admit. She had seen a Stetson in the window of the shop and recognised the stitch-work on the brim, to be similar to that of Hank Cartwright's hat. She therefore concluded that I was his milliner and may have a way of contacting him. On entering the shop, the Gainsborough painting had assured her of my acquaintance with Mr Cartwright.

Retrieving a newspaper clipping from below, it was my turn to tap on the counter. She took some time to study the article; a click of her tongue indicated when she had finished.

'Do you know 'is son?' She asked sharply, her demeanour, no longer benign.

'No', I replied, confident that this was not a complete untruth. Perhaps I should have again asked which one but I had an inkling she was talking about Jay. Besides I knew none of the Cartwright sons.

'But I saw you last week by the canal. You were at the Rattenbury, non?'

Finally, she had played her cards and the surprise on my face was evident. One, that she had been following me, and two that she had told me. Her lip turned in a smile.

'So you know 'im, yes?' She had continued unflustered.

'No.' I stood my ground. I knew of Jay Cartwright but I did not know Jay Cartwright

'Very well', she replied, ''av it your way. I will find 'im myself.' She made a determined turn and headed for the door.

Keen for more information from this intriguing creature I ventured a further question.

'Why do you ask?'

She had shrugged and still with her back to me she turned her head slightly to reply over her shoulder.

'There is unfinished business. I thought per'aps you may 'av some too?'

Turning to face me once more, she revelled in the silence, watching for my reaction as my mind sorted through the possible replies. Why had she not known Hank Cartwright was dead? Should I tell her about Delilah? What did she know about the gallery? What was the significance of the Gainsborough and Hank Cartwright? I longed to ask more questions, but the fear of showing my hand too early and the worry of revealing more of Delilah's secrets than she had intended, prevented me from doing so.

The bell on the shop door 'ting'd as another customer entered the shop.

'Perhaps you would contact me Monsieur 'etherington, should the 'at I am after be in your possession in the future.' Walking away she smiled back at the counter and the bell 'ting'd again as she left.

I was left once more with my hats and a midweek browser. I offered him help and began the usual line of questioning; event, colour, size, et cetera et cetera, and I considered the implications of my latest meeting in this curious tale.

My overriding line of thought was: why was she trying to find Hank Cartwright? What had Hank or Jay got to do with the forged artwork? I assume it was forged, given my conversation with Delilah and the accounts that lay before me. But Delilah had also implied that the Cartwright's were kept in the dark with regards to the forged artwork and that Hank and Jay were no longer communicating. Was this a ruse? Were they in fact in business together?

This of course led to more questions: If Mademoiselle Derenne lived in France permanently, as

I suspected, then had she made this trip specifically to find Hank Cartwright? Or perhaps she was trying to find Jay through his father?

And yet more: why had she been unable to find the youngest Cartwright when she clearly knew where he lived? Perhaps she did not know him? Or was he was avoiding her? Did he even know she was looking for him?

So there I was again in a sea of assumption with no real paddle of truth or fact.

As I held up a sapphire blue trilby with matching satin band for the consideration of my browser, I decided it was finally time to track down the elusive Jay Cartwright and I was pretty sure I knew where to find him.

The Breton

The austere frontage of the Wentlock Arms dates back to the Regency period, with canal barge green sash windows that are peeling from years of wear and tear. The door is solid oak and, on this particular evening, it stood ajar, inviting passers-by into the porch and the tavern-style bar inside.

The current owners have resisted modernisation, leaving the floorboards bare and the bar somewhat rough and ready; if you move too quickly you may receive a splinter from the bar or a stool.

The Wentlock Arms on a Friday night was unsurprisingly busy; although it didn't take me long to locate the infamous Jay Cartwright. A brief nod from the barman in his general direction revealed a figure lounging on a high-backed bar stool, one hand on his beer, the other propping himself up as he socialised with fellow punters - what one might call a 'bar-fly'.

As I approached him there was an overwhelming smell of soap and aftershave. His hair was carefully styled in what can only be described as a haystack. The tousled look ladies seem to go mad for these days. On the back of his stool, dangling precariously from what I believe is called the 'ear' of the upright (it's amazing what I learnt from my late wife's WI) he'd hung a Breton.

The Breton is an interesting hat; it is not something that is normally embellished, but more of a functional piece. I don't tend to sell them as there's not a lot of call for them amongst my customers, but they certainly have their place in millinery books. The French make the best Bretons of course and they should always be made with wool.

On some wearers the Breton can imply dominance only associated with the captain of a ship; however, The

Rattenbury was hardly a ship. A reefer jacket was also draped over the chair, completing the ensemble. I wondered if perhaps Jay Cartwright's choice in attire was more to do with statement than function. This man wanted to convey a certain image, however incongruous.

Jay Cartwright had his back to me, so it was his acquaintance that first noticed my presence. His friend sensed a stranger in their midst and smiled a toothy grin. A brute of a man, he slugged his beer and gave me another flash of his gold tooth as Jay Cartwright turned to see the cause of his friends amusement. I supposed an older gentleman in a suit and cravat was an unexpected sight in these parts.

I gave my name and introduced myself as a friend of his father. He didn't move at all from his seat as he appraised me. Eventually, he waved a hand toward an empty stool between him and his friend and asked if I would like to join them for a beer. I declined, but offered to buy him one if we could talk alone for a moment, to which he consented perhaps a little too readily. The implication being perhaps, that this man was used to clandestine meetings and nefarious business dealings in his local pub? He gave his friend a sharp instruction to get the next round in ready for his return.

Pulling his jacket from the chair, he walked towards the back of the pub and I followed. Immediately outside the back door was a small yard surrounded by a wall, the lapping water of the canal could be heard just the other side. Jay had brought his half supped pint to ward against the wintry chill and I was glad of my leather gloves and thick scarf.

'So what do you want, old man?' His breath fogged the air as he spoke and his Texas drawl was not at all like his father's. He was deliberate and yet casual at the same time. Leaning against the wall of the pub, one leg bent up, he balanced his beer on one of the windowsills behind him and lit up a cigarette.

This was not the sort of greeting I was used to but then again Jay Cartwright was not a person I would normally find myself conversing with. However sometimes a man has to swallow his pride in order to receive the reward.

'I was sorry to hear about your father's untimely death....'

'Yeah, yeah, yeah.' I was interrupted, 'Cut the crap will you, if you knew him, then you'd have known we didn't get on.'

His coarseness put me off my stride. This coupled with the unshaven stubble that gave him a distinctly unkempt look, meant I pondered Miss Delibes' reasons for entering into an engagement with this man. I quickly discarded these thoughts, they were not constructive in this situation and a woman's mind was not for me to try and unravel; however, the connection between Jay Cartwright, his father and our French art dealer was. For a moment I considered revealing my meeting with Miss Delibes, but I thought better of it.

I rallied and drew myself up once more continuing:

'Nonetheless, I am sorry for your loss. My reason for coming here this evening, is that I have had a visit from a lady who is very keen to see you and, as a friend of your father, I felt it my duty to advise you of this fact.'

'Did you now? And who might this lady be Mr Hetherington?'

'A Mademoiselle Derenne.' I watched his face intently for any kind of twitch, or crease that might indicate his thoughts. Nothing.

'And is there anything else you feel it is your duty you should tell me, as such a good friend of my father's?'

It was now very clear, Jay Cartwright was a taker not a giver, finding him had been the easy bit, but I was going to have to find another way of discovering his connection with Mademoiselle Derenne. From where I was standing, I could see only one weakness in this man.

'Perhaps a whiskey would help against the cold?' I offered 'then we can talk some more about your connection with the French art dealer'.

'Why are you so interested?'

Curious as to the significance of the painting that had raised the interest of at least three of the customer's in this tale, I tried a different tack.

'Art is an interest of mine, especially Thomas Gainsborough's paintings.'

There was not a flicker of recognition about Cartwright's face. He didn't move a muscle, save to take another drag on his cigarette. Unfortunately, my new assertiveness had not paid off. Tilting his head and smirking, his eyes now searched my face for my weakness. He pushed himself off the wall with the foot of his bent leg and took a step closer, leaning forward slightly:

'You're out of your depth old man; go home before you say something you regret.'

His breath cut through the aroma of Imperial Leather, engulfing me in the smell of stale beer and cigarettes. From this distance I could see each one of his capped and whitened teeth glinting in the moonlight. He was right; this was a long way from millinery. There is no embellishment available that can cover the inappropriately sized ego.

The silence was palpable, stretching out into the night. Grinding his cigarette butt into the paving slabs, he turned and walked back into the pub. There was no point in following. Sixty-plus years of dealing with stroppy young men had taught me that much. The question remained though; why was Jay Cartwright so determined to keep his association with Mademoiselle Derenne a mystery?

Exiting the yard, I picked up the towpath beyond and began to make my way homeward, pondering the events of the last few weeks. I listed the facts in my head:

—   *A plutocratic banker drowned in the canal - death by misadventure?*

—   *A millionaire rancher and able horseman thrown from his steed - accidental death?*

—   *The whispered conversation of Bollinger and Gargano - friends or foes?*

—   *The intriguing request of Miss Delibes regarding her mother's disappearance - missing or lying low?*

—   *And finally, Miss Derenne's unfinished business?*

There had to be a link!

A disturbance in the water broke my thoughts; mallards out for a late night paddle. I saw The Rattenbury ahead of me. Its mooring ring squeaked, the damp heavy warp pulling against it as the barge rocked gently in the water. At either end were moored two other barges both humming with the social activity of evening meals. With no lights on at all, The Rattenbury took on a much more sinister appearance. In darkness, barges are not so inviting.

As I came level with the barge I noticed the door ajar: a careless error for a seemingly careful owner. Surely the neighbourly thing to do would be to pull it shut, protecting the inside from prying eyes and the elements? It would take me a minute to do and, who knows, Cartwright might even thank me for it and make himself more amenable?

As I stepped down onto the deck, the barge lurched and I briefly found myself standing with my arms outstretched eyes fixed on the deck trying to find my sea legs. Once balanced, I looked up at the small door leading to the cabin. The wood was splintered and the paintwork cracked in what was to me an obvious forced entry.

By now you know that I am a gentleman of good moral standing and community spirit, so one might expect me to have called the police; I did not. Curiosity got the better of me again and what I did next was most out of character.

The Deer Stalker

Pushing the door open a little further, I was able to see into the gloom of the cabin. The curtains were drawn throughout but chinks of moonlight split the darkness in places. Rather than turning on the lights in the cabin and risk alerting the neighbours, to my presence, I was after all trespassing, I used a small pocket torch. Thankfully, I always carry the torch as my residence, unlike my shop, is comparatively rural and on occasion there have been power cuts. The small light allowed me to illuminate the room in patches and, painfully aware that Cartwright may return at any minute, but hoping the lure of beer would keep him there at least until last orders, I took in what I could of each room.

As I made my way through the barge, I was able to piece together the scene. A combination of bachelor living and what appeared to be a frantic search combined to make an angry mess. To accompany the chaos there was an overwhelming smell of cigarettes mingled with that of a decaying pot plant.

The initial living space was cluttered and cramped; I could see why Miss Delibes had declined to live in such conditions. A small bench seat was hidden under a pile of discarded coats and hats. A hunting jacket lay on the top of the pile, accompanying a deerstalker, clearly indicating Cartwright's preference with regard to his spare time.

I paused for a moment to consider the deerstalker. We are all familiar with the famous Sherlock Holmes and one can hardly fail to see a deerstalker without it invoking the image of an eccentric detective and his trusty friend. This deerstalker was a more modern version. Made from checked fabric with faux fur lined side flaps, this hat was the sort of mass-produced nonsense I would not sell in my shop.

Further in was the galley kitchen, which housed a stack of unwashed dishes and mugs. One may have been forgiven for assuming a family of four lived on this small barge as opposed to one man. As I panned the torch across the kitchen area I discovered, on the draining board, an ashtray similar to those found in the Wentlock arms. It was piled high with cigarette butts and poking out from underneath I could just make out the end of a Cuban cigar.

My heart raced as I realised the significance of my first real clue. Things were beginning to fall into place. Could a meeting with Jay Cartwright have been the reason for Henry Bollinger's stroll along the canal? Assuming this was the case and that Mr Cartwright had not cleaned out the ashtray for weeks (please be assured, that this is what it looked like) could this be the cigar of Henry Bollinger?

I scanned the cupboards above for a suitable receptacle and found what I was looking for. Conveniently for me, a roll of freezer bags was protruding from a cupboard. I carefully removed the cigar butt with my gloved hand. Pausing to sniff it, I could smell the same familiar aromas that used to rise from Mr Bollinger's jacket on his visits to the shop.

As I placed the cigar butt into a freezer bag I absorbed the significance of the canal, Bollinger, Cartwright and the cigar. For a moment I was lost in the smell of the tightly rolled, dried, and fermented tobacco.

Bursting out of the silence, a raucous laugh came from one of the barges. Proverbially leaping out of my skin, I seriously considered turning back. But I had to look further; I owed it to my recently deceased customers and, most of all, Miss Delibes. She had, after all, asked for my help.

As I moved past the shower room the smell of Imperial Leather hung in the air once more, creating a brief sanctuary in the malodorous barge. The next room was the bedroom, even more dark and chaotic than those rooms preceding it. The doors to the tiny cupboard were wide open; clothes and seat cushions covered the small floor space.

Walking into the room, I was careful as to where I put my feet. I paused to shine the torch into the cupboard and the light glinted off a metal object. On closer inspection this was a rifle, in keeping with the hunting paraphernalia present in the stern of the boat.

Another thought nagged at me. Hank Cartwright's horse had been scared by gunfire, resulting in the rancher's accidental death. Could this be the rifle that fired the shot? At that point I told myself to stop being ridiculous: I was a milliner, not a detective. A deerstalker, a cigar butt and now a rifle, what on earth was I doing here anyway? But intrigue was upon me again and I moved forward into the bow of the boat.

Panning the torch away from the rifle and back into the room in front of me, I was surprised to discover another room. This was the only room in the boat where the curtains were open making it easier for me to see as the moonlight glinted off the contents of the cabin. It was a very small room, comprising of two bench seats underneath large windows that looked out onto a small deck.

The cushions of the seats had been removed, presumably the cushions currently littering the bedroom floor next door. The wooden tops of the seats had also been removed revealing capacious storage below. The floor to the cabin had been dismantled to allow storage in the hull. This had been lined with plastic, perhaps to stop the damp from the canal encroaching on the contents.

The only clue as to what this compartment once held was some empty picture frames. Some of them seemed to have been artificially aged, although in the moonlight, even enhanced with my torch, it made it difficult to tell. Here and there, the occasional fragment of canvas was still attached to the frames.

There were approximately ten in total ranging in size. Finally my torchlight rested on a lone canvas at the bottom of one of the compartments. Still with my gloves on I leaned in and retrieved it. Unrolling it I was greeted by the serene face of the Duchess of Devonshire.

From behind me there was a cough, and I froze as I heard the click of Jay Cartwright's rifle.

'I told you to go home, old man...'

The Custodian

Beads of sweat began to form on my forehead; I had gone too far. I should have turned around when I'd found the cigar end. This was, indeed, no place for a milliner. My mind played over the options, of which there were not many.

Jay had me at a distinct disadvantage. I had heard that it is harder to kill someone who is facing you and the fact that I had my back to him increased his advantage further. However, I also knew that a rifle makes a lot of noise. He would surely be foolish to fire it in such confined quarters and so close to those who might hear.

I was, unfortunately, correct.

'Turn around, we're going for a walk.' He continued.

As I turned to face him I rolled the fake Gainsborough up again.

'As you know, I've always been an admirer of the Gainsborough,' I smiled. 'It's the sheer audacity of the hat you see; all that pomp and circumstance. It can give the wearer an air of elegance not found under other hats.' Engaging him in conversation surely couldn't make it any worse.

'You can leave that where you found it.' He pointed the rifle in the direction of the bench seats.

'What do you hope to achieve by killing me Jay?' I replied, as I put the painting back into its hiding place.

'Who says I'm gonna kill ya?' His face was hidden in the darkness of the bedroom, but I could tell, from his voice, he was smirking.

'I'm afraid that the gun pointed at me gives me an indication of your intention and I know you've killed before,' I replied.

'Have I? Maybe I'll just kneecap ya, hey? Who's going to believe the ramblings of a batty old man in a wheelchair?'

He had a point. I didn't really have any firm evidence and I was walking a fine line. I had no idea what may cause this man to snap.

Slowly I put my hands in my pockets. They fell first on the cigar butt, reminding me again of poor Bollinger, and then on my mobile phone. It was the one occasion I was truly thankful I had not resisted technology entirely. The mobile phone was useful for my business. People these days wanted instant contact. If the shop was closed then few were willing to wait anymore. I began to feel my way around the keypad hoping I may be able to raise the alarm in some way.

'Take your hands out of your pockets and get walking.' He took a step closer.

My only option was to oblige him and we made our way from the bow, back to the stern of the barge. I could feel the steel of the gun in my shoulder blade. Cartwright was a man who lacked subtlety so why would he start now?

As we walked back through the barge I considered grabbing a plate from the galley and bashing it over his head, but I knew he was a younger fitter man than me and this was never going to work. I had to use my brain and outwit him somehow. Perhaps I could risk jumping in the canal and making a swim for the other side?

The lights in the stern were now on, illuminating the disorder of the living space. As we crossed the last room before the door to the night outside, I felt the boat rock slightly and a voice called out from the deck.

'Jay are you there?' It was Delilah Delibes.

Cartwright stopped. I attempted to continue with the last two steps to the doorway, but the rifle pushed firmly into my shoulder blade persuaded me otherwise.

As Delilah opened the door she lent in. Her face was confused and then angry, as she squinted in the light from the cabin.

'Mr Hetherington! You have no right to be here. How could you do this…?' She gestured at the broken lock and frame.

She was quite a picture and one I shan't easily forget. Utility trousers and a mud stained fleece, had replaced her usual, fashionable attire. Her face and hair were also less manicured than I remembered from my previous encounters. So here stood the archaeologist, in the light of the Rattenbury cabin.

Jay nudged me forward with the rifle and I stepped through onto the deck. It was then that Delilah saw her fiancé.

'Jay what are you doing?' She was alarmingly calm, as if her fiancé pointing a rifle at a gentleman was normal Friday night procedure.

'Tying up a few loose ends from the look of it. Tell me, how do you know our Mr Hetherington darling?' he replied.

'I err,' pausing just a little too long, her reply was weak. 'Where else do you think I get my hats from sweetheart?'

'I think you need to come with me and Mr Hetherington, honey. I think we need a little chat, just us three, real nice like.' He had a crooked smile as he included Miss Delibes in his line of fire, only moving the rifle to indicate the bank onto which we were to step.

For a moment, as we stood on the deck, all that could be heard was the muffled conversations of the adjacent barges as Delilah processed the scene. Then, to mine and indeed Cartwright's surprise, Miss Delibes' lungs launched an assault on the ears with a scream that could have been heard in Regents Park.

Seeing my chance, I lunged forward, grabbing at the rifle. Cartwright was stronger than me but lacked experience and my school days proved useful, as my old boxing instructors words rang in my ears. Unsurprisingly, he was not keen to give the weapon up and there was a considerable struggle of which I am not altogether certain of the particulars. However, there are some pertinent points, which stick in one's memory.

A rather ridiculous do-se-do ensued and I had to be light on my feet, in an attempt to relieve Cartwright of the rifle whilst at the same time preventing it from pointing at anything alive. Finally, I managed to punch Cartwright square on the jaw, a jolly good shot if I may be permitted to say so, although to revel in this would not be gentlemanly. Throwing myself in front of Miss Delibes as the rifle discharged itself into the deck in front of her was my pièce de résistance.

By this point the combination of Delilah's scream and the rifle fire had finally roused the attention of the other barge owners and onlookers were appearing on the decks either side. Dropping the gun, Cartwright made a leap for the bank and ran into the night; after all, most bullies are proved to be cowards in the end.

Miss Delibes and I were left on the deck, shaken but in no state to give chase. A hole in the deck beneath us indicated where the shot had found its resting place. It was then that I became conscious of a burning sensation in my foot. Looking down I saw the hole in my shoe and I don't mind saying I felt a little unwell.

Delilah was tremendous, given the fact that her fiancé had just tried to murder us both. She soon had onlookers ringing the police and an ambulance, fetching brandy and even finding towels from the barge to wrap around my injured foot. It was only when all the commotion had subsided and the police had left me in the company of the paramedics and the bright lights of an ambulance, that I allowed myself to breathe a sigh of relief.

Miss Delibes had insisted on accompanying me to hospital and she sat on one of the seats opposite me telling me how sorry she was to have dragged me into this; how she should have heeded her mother's warnings and how if she ever caught up with Jay Cartwright again she'd.... well, I never did find out.

Her voice soothed my nerves as I drifted off, thinking once more on the events of the last few weeks. I wasn't entirely sure millinery alone was going to be enough for me anymore. I had been on a thrilling adventure and survived.

Epilogue

'Following his trial, Mr Jay Cartwright, son of the recently deceased millionaire Hank Cartwright, has been jailed for four years, for fraud and a further five years for grievous bodily harm.

In the course of their investigation, Scotland Yard uncovered a European smuggling ring, which allowed Cartwright to deal in fraudulent artworks. Cartwright exported the works from a gallery in London to dealers in Italy and France with the aid of a yacht, romantically named the Bel Fiore. Mr Cartwright is thought to have made thousands from selling the forged artwork.

A French art dealer has also been arrested in Paris, charged in connection with the crime and is awaiting deportation for trial in England. The police are anxious to contact Ms Flora Delibes and Signor Antony Gargano, to assist them with their enquiries.'

After a lengthy investigation, and an eventual admission of guilt in an attempt to reduce his sentence, Cartwright's web of crime finally became public knowledge. However, the newspaper article does not explain everything in this intriguing case to my satisfaction.

First of all let me address the conviction for grievous bodily harm, as I am indeed aggrieved. The sentence was not the maximum sixteen years that I am led to believe such a crime can carry, but instead a minimum sentence of five years.

Because the gun was pointing down at the time, it was judged that there was no solid evidence that Mr

Cartwright had intended to harm us. I would beg to differ. Prior to the incident the gun had definitely been pointing at Miss Delibes and myself suggesting entirely the contrary. It was, frankly, no less than attempted murder in my book.

Then of course there is the small matter of the murders that were successful!

Let me explain by taking into account the extensive circumstantial evidence I have collected in regard to the characters in this tale. This evidence clearly could not be reported in the newspaper for fear of libel.

I assume Henry Bollinger became greedy; most men will bend to one of the seven sins at some point in their life. His position as a banker perhaps meant that he saw large sums of money being deposited in Jay Cartwright's bank account. Maybe that hushed conversation between Gargano and Bollinger was regarding their mutual interest in the artwork. Could he, in fact, have decided to investigate further, leading him to the Rattenbury, the *Bel Fiore* or the gallery? Perhaps he tried to cash in on Jay's scheme or even blackmail him? If he did indeed venture either of these propositions, then this would surely explain his unfortunate dip in the canal.

As for poor Hank Cartwright, it is possible that he knew of Jay's crimes and intended to put an end to them. Maybe he had offered Derenne a pay-off in exchange for ending her dealings with his son? This may explain Mademoiselle Derenne's search for Hank Cartwright.

Unfortunately for Hank, his son made the first move. Wielding his trusty rifle once again he rid himself of an interfering father, and in the process, gained a fortune.

If we assume that the youngest Cartwright was indeed responsible for the demise of both his father and Henry Bollinger then this goes a long way to explaining his mother's reaction to the death of her husband. It is no wonder she left the country so quickly? A mother will always know her son's true nature, for she has nurtured him.

Perhaps Jay did push Bollinger into the canal and fire the gun that caused his father's horse to bolt. There is no way of proving this but I myself remain convinced that Jay Cartwright was in some way responsible for the deaths of Henry Bollinger and Hank Cartwright. I am not so convinced however, that there will ever be true justice for those that suffered and in fact lost their lives at the hands of Jay Cartwright.

I shall continue to help Miss Delibes locate her missing mother. I again assume, given the existence of the photograph and the note on the back, that Flora Delibes and Signor Gargano have left the country together to lie low, as it were. I am not hopeful of the return of either, but if we are to ever find them perhaps they will hold the key to proving Jay Cartwright's part in the aforementioned untimely deaths.

Delilah has been truly British about the whole affair. Discovering one's fiancé is a master criminal and your mother is involved to boot is enough to make anyone quiver, but not our Miss Delibes. She is a truly amazing young woman.

The artwork from the gallery was of course seized as evidence and once the police had finished with the place, Miss Delibes turned the gallery into a small museum. It now houses archaeological finds pertaining to the Roman occupation; fascinating.

Miss Delibes and I still meet every week at The Snicket where the herb-crusted scallops have become a favourite of mine. I feel it is my duty to help her in her newly orphaned state, and having a younger mind around is like a breathe of fresh air for my old soul. It is hard to be alone in this world.

Miss Delibes later explained to me, the fortunate circumstances that brought her to my aid that night on The Rattenbury. The presence of a crimson-red beret following her up the towpath, on her return from work, had meant she had sought refuge in the barge, not realising she was going from the frying pan into the fire. When Jay and I had appeared in the doorway of the barge, the red beret had disappeared into the night.

Several months on and we are able to laugh at ourselves: Hetherington and Delibes the dynamic duo, detecting the great crime of the decade. I now have a smart cane to aid me with the limp I acquired during that fateful evening.

I sometimes wish for a new puzzle to unravel but I do enjoy the peace and quiet of routine. So, for now, I wait patiently in the shop serving the regulars, perusing the papers and watching the world go by outside. After all, who knows what the future may bring; perhaps I should acquire a Trilby?

ONE FOR THE ROOK

BLAKE HETHERINGTON MYSTERY #2

'One for the rook
One for the crow
One to wither
One to grow.'

Old English rhyme circa 18th century.

The Pumpkin

Peter, Peter, pumpkin eater,
Had a wife but couldn't keep her;
He put her in a pumpkin-shell,
And there he kept her very well.

Nursery Rhyme c1825

It is often said that an Englishman's home is his castle. For me my castle is my allotment: a magnificent estate surrounded by a four-foot fence, with a strong foundation of root vegetables, a lush carpet of Cucurbita and in September golden crenellations of sweet corn. I am lucky to be the king of one hundred and twenty five metres square.

I live in the rural village of Tuesbury, just an hour's commute from London. Living in Tuesbury affords me the countryside I would so miss if I lived in the heart of London, nearer my shop. The only thing that keeps me from my allotment is my profession. The customer's enthusiasm for hat buying invariably coincides with the growing season and over the years it has left me torn between the need to grow my business and my love of growing vegetables. The events of that autumn, however, changed the history of both my business and my allotment forever.

This season, a steady stream of customers perused and purchased their way through the stock of Hetherington's Hats, from the beginning of March to the summer beyond. Off to a flying start with the Cheltenham Festival, sales gathered pace in June for the tennis at Wimbledon, and levelled out around the time of Glorious Goodwood on the Sussex Downs. It was the same every year and now we had reached the autumnal lull. The nights were starting to draw in and it wouldn't be long before the approach of the Christmas festivities, sent people into a flurry of consumerism once more.

This autumn there was a small unseasonal peak in sales aided by the glorious sunshine that accompanied the last days of September. It was the kind that demands an oversized, be-ribboned, floppy brimmed straw hat or, in my case, the humble boater. The boater really is the only dignified hat for a man of my age to protect himself from the heat of the midday sun.

Days spent in the shop were hot and stuffy and even with the air conditioning unit running full blast, my customers were listless. Despite the unpredicted boost in sales, by four o'clock most days, the customers had run dry. I must confess, on the hottest days, I often shut up shop early; one one of the joys of owning your own business. That and the horizon of retirement allows one to view life from a different angle. Why wait for a customer who was never going to arrive? They would be sitting on their balconies enjoying the last of the sun and I much prefer to spend the evenings on my allotment back home.

My allotment is one of fifty plots in the heart of the village, sandwiched in between the thatched cottages on the High Street and the old council estate on Poets Avenue. We are lucky to have such a large piece of land given over to the fashion of subsistence. In these times of austerity, when land and affordable housing is at a premium, the allotments are often under threat, but the village fights hard to keep its precious plots.

I myself have owned my allotment for twenty years and I grow a variety of fruiting bushes and vegetables, for my own table, my daughter's, and now this year Delilah's, who I'm pleased to say has taken a great interest in horticulture. Since our meeting, last year, I have developed an avuncular affection for Delilah and her company is a joy. I have often tried to interest my daughter in horticulture but I find she is preoccupied with her own family these days. A natural progression one supposes, but I digress.

I have had to learn to dig using my left foot, rather than my preferred right. The unfortunate injury I sustained last year, during my attempt to apprehend the leader of a now notorious forgery ring, still hinders me, although I am assured it will get better in time. The cane provides a little extra support. My attempt was not, however, in vain and I have become something of a local hero; not that I bask in that particular glory.

The police are still looking for the missing members of the gang, one of which is Delilah's mother. Delilah and I have almost given up hope of them ever returning to this country. I'm not sure whether poor Delilah wishes it or not. Well over a year has passed now and I feel sure they have settled in sunnier climes, safe from extradition. In fact our story starts almost exactly a year from the events that unfolded on the Regent's Canal last year! What is it that makes September such a murderous month? But, again, I stray from my purpose.

Whilst I am gardening, my cane rests beside the shed that stands on my allotment, as it has for many years. It is a good size for a shed and I have resisted downsizing, in favour of more space to grow vegetables, as it is a pleasant refuge. It also houses some of my gardening books, a little DAB radio, gardening tools, tins of seeds and, of course, a good supply of slug pellets.

And so we come to the tenants of our little Eden. We are lucky to have fifty allotments in Tuesbury but I will only introduce you to a few. To introduce fifty would result in a story of epic proportions.

Having grown up in Tuesbury, I am very familiar with its residents, especially as my late wife was a very active member of the community. She was a member of the Women's Institute, the St Mary's Church Flower Arrangers and was also a Tawny Owl at the local girl guides. As a result, the villagers also know me; the one and only downside to living in such a small community.

We are not without our criminal fraternity on the allotments - although I am not one to gossip. Samphire Devine owns the plot next door to mine and is the wife of the notorious Reuben Devine, head of the *'Devine's Diablos'*, a burglary gang that targeted high class properties. But that was some years ago now and he is currently languishing in Wandsworth Prison.

Mrs Devine keeps herself to herself in the main, only ever stopping to chat with Delilah when their visits to the allotments coincide. In fact Delilah would often go for a drink with Samphire, if she'd been at the allotment for the day. I of course did not approve given Delilah's inexplicable attraction to the criminal underworld, but I should not judge.

The Devines' plot is smaller than my own but Samphire only seems to grow wildflowers. I'm not entirely sure if that is by accident or design. It does mean I am forever pulling rosebay willowherb from my vegetable beds, which can become very tedious.

Mary Ananassa owns plot number seven. She is seldom seen but often heard, banging pots and pans in her ramshackle caravan. Like myself, she was born in the village. She is from a long line of Romanies and her allotment is a cluttered affair. In the corner of it stands the caravan. Its awning has been converted into a flimsy greenhouse where she grows a plethora of Aloe vera and cacti. The rest of her plot is a very eclectic mix of what can only be described as medicinal plants. In the evenings the strangest smells waft from the caravan windows, presumably from whatever concoctions, cocktails and potions she is brewing from these plants.

On noticing my limp, Ms Ananassa once made the grave error of trying to sell me a herbal cure for arthritis. Needless to say she has not broached the subject again. Since this exchange, though, we have become acquainted over various cups of herbal tea, while seated outside her caravan in the dusk of the evening. She tells me about the healing powers of plants and I enjoy the evening air and a chance to relax after an afternoon's digging.

One tenant I do my best to avoid is Mrs Olea Faba. An incorrigible gossip, she is quite the opposite of Mary. I pity her poor husband, whose shoulders are often slumped and resigned to whatever verbal chastisement he is subjected. Olea runs a tight ship on her allotment with not an inch of space wasted. Often taking home the lion's share of rosettes from the Tuesbury Autumn Show, she spends hours weeding, hoeing, watering and indeed talking to her beloved vegetables.

Many of the allotment owners padlock and even chain their sheds closed. It has been known for boys from the neighbouring villages to raid the sheds for items to sell at car boots or just simply to entertain themselves. During the winter, owners have often arrived to find their vegetables trampled and their tools missing. Some have even gone so far as to attach a CCTV camera to the outside their shed. I myself have not bothered with CCTV or chains. A padlock seems to suffice. It is perhaps the absence of such paraphernalia, which results in the criminal minds deciding my shed has nothing of real value housed in it.

Finally, there is one last set of residents that I want to tell you about. For many years Tuesbury allotments had had a thriving rookery, occupying the trees on the edge of the wood bordering the most northerly plots. Their calls were strangely comforting and had become so much a part of the allotments that it was some days before their absence was noted.

For almost two weeks in August, people had commented on how quiet the allotments had become, but no one actually noticed the rookery had gone. When they did, there was much sucking of teeth, tutting and shaking of heads. The loss of a rookery is never a good omen. It is a well-known fact that if an estate loses its rookery, misfortune will follow. The estate in this case was the Tuesbury allotments.

It is here that we come to the events that befell our plots that autumn. The real trouble started during those hazy, heavy, humid days of September sun, when an intriguing series of events unravelled, the blame for which I will land firmly at the feet of the missing rookery.

There had been a terrible hullabaloo concerning a right-of-way, which purportedly ran straight across our plots. The leader of this cacophony, one Dennis Nyeman, is known in the village as being a cantankerous and asinine troublemaker.

Thrown out of the caged-bird society for creating a ruckus that almost ended in a fistfight, this year he turned his hand to ancient rights-of-way. Unfortunately, for the good burghers of Tuesbury allotments, he had rather more support on this subject than initially anticipated. This came in the form of the local rambling association.

Nyeman had of course chosen the busiest time of year on the allotments, to start the row. The Tuesbury Allotment Society Autumn Show was fast approaching and I was growing pumpkins for the yearly competition. I had chosen a variety called Hundredweight. As its name suggests, Hundredweight is one of the bigger varieties of Curcurbita. I had to work hard as they need a phenomenal amount of water; not the easiest plant to manage during a hosepipe ban.

Pumpkins are a favourite of mine despite their very non-British origins. They were brought to Britain by one of the first explorers of the new world, namely Columbus. It is said that the Native Indians showed the Pilgrim Fathers how to grow pumpkins between their crops of corn, which prevented them from starving in the winter and pumpkin pie features at the thanksgiving dinner celebrated in America. It's a thought that makes me smile when I see the humble pumpkin growing on my plot.

The more I learn about the pumpkin, the more interesting it becomes. It is no longer just a big orange gourd carved out to scare spirits on Hallows Eve. Delilah had shown an interest in the pumpkins too and I had given her a few plants on my allotment, which she tended with admirable diligence. She provides a welcome diversion as I weed and rotavate between the plants. Her speed of speech has not slowed and her voice has become a familiar feature up at the allotments. When she is not there I miss my gardening companion and her interesting facts.

'Giant pumpkins were the staple food of the Peruvian Incas, Blake', she told me one day. *'Perhaps our pumpkins shall rival those that fed our ancestors?'* And she laughed merrily at her own wit.

The increasing presence of Dennis Nyeman's demonstrations, my commitments in the shop and the heat of the day, meant I often restricted my visits to the early mornings or late evenings. Saturday was a particularly hot day. As I set off from home that morning, the weather report informed me that temperatures were set to reach a dizzying thirty degrees Celsius.

It was still very early as I arrived at the allotments and the birds were busy performing their morning songs. Despite the hour, the humidity was already too much to work in but the pumpkins needed watering. The need to maintain the growth of my Hundredweights was paramount. That year I was determined not to be pipped to the post again by Mrs Olea Faba and her Curcurbita extraordinaire. Plot thirty-one is easily viewed from my own and I was proud to say my pumpkins were doing very well in comparison. But, as they say, pride comes before a fall.

The sleeves of my shirt were rolled up to my armpits and I was not wearing my usual cravat. In fact the button on my collar was undone, the only concession I will make when the weather is this hot. I will not, under any circumstances, remove my shirt. Why the youth of today feel the need to display in such a way is beyond me. As far as I'm concerned, no lady wishes to have that view visited upon her and I was, in fact, meeting Delilah at the allotment that morning.

I was halfway down the little path between my plot and Mrs Devine's before I saw the catastrophe that awaited me. The smell of the soil, fresh with dew from the night before, was interrupted with the sweet smell of pumpkins. It was this smell that alerted me to the problem. You see pumpkins don't smell of anything until you open them up.

My efforts had been focused on three pumpkins in particular and the biggest of the three now seemed to have an addition. Peter Kürbis, owner of plot number six, directly opposite mine, was lying face down in my prize pumpkin.

Kürbis was a man in his late forties and, when not on his allotment, he could often be found in the local hostelries. I had very little knowledge of Mr Kürbis and no idea of his profession, if indeed he had one, and I had rarely spoken to him despite the proximity of our allotments. What I did know about the man, I had learnt from Delilah who occasionally frequented The Badgers' Holt, a pub on the High Street in the village. His visits to the allotments were mainly at weekends and he gave the impression of a loud and confident man, brash and cocky. He grew easy crops such as potatoes, radishes, lettuce and runner beans.

Kürbis was wearing jeans and a t-shirt; not unreasonable attire for a night out. His shoes were smart enough but the soles were worn, suggesting he often walked home. A good indication then that he may have been taking a short cut through the allotments, onto Poets Avenue.

Given the facts at my disposal, at first I thought he was drunk. It was after all Saturday morning. Maybe Friday night drinking had got the better of him and he'd fallen and somehow smashed my pumpkin, knocking himself out in the process. Hundredweight pumpkins are not something you should argue with; especially not with your head.

To say I was a little agitated by this occurrence would not quite cover my emotions at that moment in time. Five long months of careful nurturing: potting, repotting, mulching and watering had been obliterated.

I moved forward to wake him from his slumber amongst the aforementioned vegetable and berate him for his carelessness. But, as I approached, I realised that he had not, as I initially thought, hit the pumpkin; the pumpkin had hit him! It had split in half in what must have been a forcible blow. The flesh of the vegetable encompassed Peter's head in an array of orange mush, spattered with blood spots, which I assumed were the victim's.

My heart beat a little faster and my hand trembled as I crouched by his prone figure. At that angle I could see

63

a straw coloured fluid, tinged with pink had congealed in his ears, and my stomach tightened. My daughter is a nurse and frequently regales me with gruesome tales during our weekly phone conversations. It is her I have to thank for the fact that I knew that this indicated a serious head injury.

Many thoughts went through my mind. Guilt that I had thought him drunk, annoyance that he had destroyed my prize pumpkin and finally unease as I realized I had no idea what to do next. Reaching a tentative hand around the side of his neck, I felt for his carotid artery, but his cold, marbled skin told me all I needed to know. He was dead; very dead.

'Blake, what are you doing down there?' Delilah had appeared, her cheeks rosy from the humid morning air. There was a pause as she took a moment to take in the scene. 'Is that Peter? She added, and then with a little gasp, 'Is that your prize pumpkin?'

'You had better call the police, Delilah' I replied. 'I think Mr Kürbis has finally met his maker.'

The Artichoke

Seduced by Zeus, the mortal Cynara became his lover and Zeus made her a goddess; but she became homesick and returned to Earth. On her return to Olympus, Zeus was enraged by her actions and threw her back to Earth where he transformed her into an artichoke.

The police cordoned off my allotment and impounded my pumpkins as evidence. I'm afraid to say, I was sulking in the most ungentlemanly manner and I had decided to take the morning off work. I needed a strong espresso to deal with the shock of losing my prize Curcurbita. In fact, I was drinking a double.

'Well, I'll never be able listen to Smashing Pumpkins again.' Delilah said. She chuckled as she scooped up the froth from her cappuccino.

Delilah's blasé attitude towards death never ceased to amaze me. I supposed that surrounding herself with ancient disasters, artefacts and corpses may have a desensitising effect. Nevertheless, first impressions are difficult to shake off. On our first meeting, the ridiculous hatinator and loyal little dog had made her seem so vulnerable; how could I have refused the help she requested? Little did I know, this trowel-wielding archaeologist was more than capable of fending for herself.

We'd chosen to have coffee at Frascati: an eccentric little Italian café on the High Street across the road from the allotments. Its plastic tablecloths in red, white and green, gave a *'village fete beer tent'* feel to the place. The chairs were high backed and wholly uncomfortable but for some reason Delilah liked it here. She said it reminded her of a little café she'd once visited in Pompeii. She said if she closed her eyes whilst drinking her coffee, the warmth that emanated from the kitchen made her feel like she was on holiday again. On a day like today one didn't need to imagine all that much; the heat was stifling.

There were a few places that opened early for breakfast in Tuesbury, one of which served very nice almond croissants. Not Frascati though. Frascati was particularly famous for its '*All Day Breakfast Calzone*'. Not something I ever intend to try. Why on earth would you surround fried eggs, beans, mushrooms, bacon and sausages with pizza dough?

Frascati extended their trade at the other end of the day by offering take-away pizzas, which were very popular with the locals. I frequently found empty pizza boxes stuffed in my composter; most inconvenient.

'Who do you think did it then?' Delilah asked eagerly.

I looked at Delilah's expectant face. She'd been restless since last September but I assumed it was the disappearance of her mother rather than the desire for another mystery to solve. Wrong again. I wasn't used to being this wrong about a person and perhaps that's why I enjoy Delilah's company. I can expect the unexpected.

I had no idea who was responsible for the demise of my pumpkin and of course Mr Kürbis. I had actually been sitting there wondering what state my allotment was going to be in by the time the police finished. Some of the crops were not so much of a worry. I had plenty of onions drying in the shed and most of the beans had gone over now. Even so, the sweet corn was nowhere near ripe.

I had left the forensic team crouched in amongst the crop of Sundance, dismantling the water butt. Lord knows how many of my vegetables would survive the onslaught. There had been mutterings of compensation and forms to sign but, at the end of the day, they had an unexplained death on their hands. My corn on the cob was hardly going to be top of their priorities.

'I didn't really know Mr Kürbis', I replied stirring a lump of brown sugar into my espresso. Perhaps a double had been a little over the top. But I was still sulking. 'He seemed decent enough to me. A little coarse in his language perhaps, but that's hardly worth murder, is it?'

Delilah shrugged and I watched her devour the last of the breakfast calzone. The morning's events had certainly given her an appetite. Watching her eating the pseudo-Italian atrocity, made my stomach growl and I longed for an almond croissant, but it was not to be.

'What about Dennis Nyeman? He's a surly fellow, ' Delilah finally replied, wiping her mouth with a dark green napkin. 'I've always thought he was a little bit psychotic,' she rotated her finger near her temple, 'and the corner of Peter's allotment is part of that ancient right-of-way he's crowing over.' She pushed her plate forward and folded her arms giving me a satisfied look.

'He does have a predilection for violence I suppose.' I said as I sipped my espresso.

'Wasn't there that incident a while back with Fred Carstairs?'

Delilah was referring to the infamous occasion when Fred Carstairs, chairman of the caged bird society, dared to suggest Nyeman should feed his birds on higher quality millet. I understand he found himself in A & E with a broken nose.

'Well yes.' I replied placing my tiny cup back on its tiny saucer.

'See, I told you', Delilah replied, triumphant. 'Wrapped up in no time! Delibes and Hetherington strike again. Perhaps we should go and tell the police!' She grinned.

I lent forward pulling myself out of my morose cloud of pumpkin-pity. Before continuing the conversation, I pushed the vase, containing a plastic red rose, to one side. I have no idea why they put those things on the table, it not only clutters valuable eating space but it interferes with the conversation.

'But, why Peter?' I replied. 'There are several allotments that the right-of-way passes through. Surely Nyeman would have murdered us all by now if that was the case?'

'Maybe this is just the start' Delilah replied with a little too much enthusiasm for my liking.

I chose to ignore her rather macabre proposition and instead tried to find a rather more sensible answer than the idea of Nyeman marching about in the middle of the night, leaving the bodies of hapless allotment owners in his wake.

'So if it was Nyeman, as you are so keen to believe, what was he doing up there in the middle of the night?' I asked Delilah.

Delilah paused for a moment, picked up a toothpick and started digging around in her teeth for stray pieces of calzone.

'I 'on't expec' a 'ad'an 'hinks 'uch a'out 'he 'ime.' She replied.

Just about decoding the tooth picked words I replied; 'But Nyeman, is not a madman, he does his meddling during the day. He prefers an audience.'

'He's hardly going to want an audience for murder though Blake', Delilah replied incredulously. Thankfully she had dispensed with the toothpick. She was right, no murderer wants an audience. Perhaps this was just the beginning of some kind of murderous plot to gain the right-of-way back from the allotment owners. It was still the high-risk strategy of a lunatic and I wasn't entirely convinced.

'And what was Kürbis doing up there?' I said, 'I assumed he was walking home but...' my words trailed off. I was still stuck on the crazed madman theory. Nyeman was annoying yes, but he really wasn't a psychopath.

'Oh come on Blake, you're over-thinking things again. Nyeman's a brute. It must have been him. He's one section away from crazy and this time he's gone too far.' Delilah finished her tirade as Ed, the owner of the little café, came to collect her empty plate and resting cutlery.

As English as the day is long, it was Ed's great grandmother that was Italian. He was not. Of average height and build, Ed had dark hair and grey eyes. Not an unattractive man for his age, but he had definitely let himself slip in terms of fitness. His burgeoning waistline and pale complexion were perhaps the result of long days in the kitchen, surrounded by food and a distinct lack of sun. It was nothing that couldn't easily be fixed by a good walk in the countryside.

Today his white, half apron, was smeared with tomato and flour and his forehead was beaded with sweat. I was very glad I had forgone breakfast.

'What's going on over there?' Ed nodded in the direction of the allotments. You can't directly see the plots from the café, just the hedges surrounding them and the small gate that led onto the plots from the High Street. However, today the gate had the attention of a policeman and the addition of some iconic blue and white tape that fluttered in the breeze.

I looked at Delilah. She knew I hated to gossip but the pause in the conversation must have been too long for Ed.

'Come on, what's going on? Don't leave me hanging here.' He gesticulated in the direction of the allotments with the empty plate, the cutlery rattling in agreement.

'Well, you may as well know...' Delilah started.

I coughed, attempting to prevent an indiscretion. I wasn't sure how much we were supposed to know. Delilah looked at me with an exasperated expression. In truth we had just been discussing Mr Kürbis' unfortunate demise over breakfast in a very public place. I sighed, shrugged and Delilah continued.

'Peter Kürbis has been murdered' she said, savouring the word 'murdered'.

'No!' Ed said. 'How?'

'Pumpkin to the head; splat!' Delilah replied bringing the palm of her hand down on the table with a little too much enthusiasm.

'Not your prize pumpkin Mr Hetherington, surely?' Ed replied, turning towards me.

I nodded. I did not need reminding.

'Murdered? But he wasn't that bad?' This amused me as it implied Ed might consider murder appropriate if the victim was a real cad.

'Sure,' Ed continued, 'he was a player, but, what red-blooded male isn't if he can get away with it? Live and let live I say.' He busied himself collecting my unused cutlery.

'Peter had a girlfriend!?' Delilah was incredulous.

'Yeah, of course he did.' Ed replied.

Peter Kürbis was not short of admirers and it had surprised me that Delilah had not fallen for his charms. Again, I found myself wondering if she was perhaps more astute than I gave her credit for.

'But he was a total misogynist! He never had a civil word for me.' Delilah replied. And there it was, the truth of the matter. Peter Kürbis was what one might call a man's man and, intimidated by Delilah's intelligence, chose not to woo her but instead to make derogatory remarks.

'Well from where I was standing, he very much liked women.' Ed replied 'He often came in here on his way back from The Badgers' Holt and you'll never guess who he was with the other night.' Ed didn't wait for a reply. 'Samphire Devine', he stepped back from the table a little, awaiting our response.

This was indeed an interesting fact. Nonetheless, this revelation was not completely surprising. Days spent up at the allotments meant I had learned a little about Mrs Devine, not a lot but a little, and sometimes a little is more than enough. You see Mrs Devine is an artichoke: Cynara herself.

From observing Mrs Devine and my conversations with Delilah, I had concluded that Samphire was very clearly *'high maintenance'*. The artichoke requires careful attention and takes two years to fully mature into an edible plant. Samphire Devine also required attention in order for her to blossom.

With her husband in prison, it was no surprise to me that she was seeking other outlets for this attention. Unfortunately, like the artichoke, Mrs Devine could be prickly if handled incorrectly. Reuben Devine must have had to work hard to keep his wife in the way she had become accustomed, but while the cat's away…

Ed and Delilah were as deep in conversation as I was in thought, and I realised it was already eleven o' clock. I had to open the shop at some point today. If I hurried, I could get the eleven forty-five into London and be ready for the afternoon trade.

'I have to get back to the shop', I said and stood up from the table. Ed and Delilah looked a little startled as my sudden action interrupted their conversation. I placed the money for the bill under the salt cellar and took my cane from the umbrella stand, 'Hats don't sell themselves you know!' I smiled.

'I'll come with you', Delilah said. 'I have some things to do in the city.' Now Ed definitely looked put out. I could see he had rather a soft spot for Delilah. She, on the other hand, had not noticed that her calzones and cappuccinos were definitely fuller than the average customer's.

'I thought perhaps you wouldn't mind staying here.' I suggested. 'That way you could keep an eye on the allotment for me and check there's not too much damage being done. That is if you don't mind?' I needed some time to think, and the train into London often gave me the perfect opportunity to mull over the little quandaries life presents; although this was more than a little quandary.

'Ok' she conceded 'I'll try to make sure they don't do too much damage, although I can't make any guarantees. There's something about men when they start digging, they get all territorial.'

Ed perked up a bit. 'Would you like another cappuccino Delilah? On the house. It must have been a shock for you finding Peter like that.'

'Well, Blake found him,' Delilah replied, but Ed was already behind the counter starting up the coffee machine.

'So what are you thinking Blake? I can tell you're onto something.' Delilah said, grinning at me.

'If I'm honest, I'm not sure what to think, but what I definitely know is you should try to stay out of trouble Miss Delibes', I smiled back at her. It was hard not to.

'At last, another mystery for us to get our teeth into! Oooh! Perhaps one of the CCTVs on someone's shed has caught some of the action. If one did, we could have this all wrapped up by dinner time.'

'I mean it Delilah. Stay out of trouble. Let the police do their job, just make sure they don't destroy all of our pumpkins.' I wagged my finger at her. This is not something I do regularly, but this was a finger wagging moment. I had a vision of Delilah scaling sheds in an attempt to retrieve the security cameras and discover the murderer. The police would not take kindly to amateur detectives, destroying a crime scene. You don't need to be Miss Marple to know this.

Ed returned with the coffee and sat down opposite Delilah. Hunching his shoulders, he leant forward conspiratorially, 'So tell me all about it - I want to know everything,' Ed said.

As I left the little pizzeria I could hear them gabbling away at a million miles an hour. Delilah was in her element and I was in mine.

I caught the eleven forty-five and found peace and quiet at last in which to think. There were too many questions and not enough answers. What had Peter Kürbis been doing on the allotments in the middle of the night and why was he killed on my allotment? Was Dennis Nyeman really capable of murder? Did Reuben Devine know about his wife's dalliance? Finally, how was I ever going to grow a pumpkin big enough to win that competition?

The Goosegrass

From the family Rubiaceae, *Galium aparine,* or goosegrass as it is more commonly known, is sometimes used as a medicinal plant for its diuretic qualities. As it grows it drags surrounding plants down with its hooked sticky leaves. Goosegrass is prolific, persistent and often considered a weed.

Delilah made a valiant attempt to limit the damage to my vegetables but the officers involved had indeed become a little territorial and asked her to leave the allotments. She had been forced to oblige, after all no-one wishes to risk incarceration, even for the sake of a prize-winning gourd. That would be foolhardy.

Sunday, day five of our mini heat wave, was spent trying to repair the damage the forensic team had caused to my plot. I do not like to criticise our boys in blue but I fully understand why they are often referred to as flat-footed. My radishes, a normally plucky and resilient catch crop, were rendered a shadow of their former selves. Blue and white cordoning tape was still present on the sweet corn and the pumpkins were definitely in shock.

Monday in the shop was hotter still. The air conditioning unit was on the opposite side of the shop to the counter and did not stretch its cool fingers of air far enough to meet my fevered brow; surely an error in design. So I stood behind the counter basking in the cool air of an oscillating fan.

There had been few customers in the shop that morning and so I chose to browse through the paper and drink iced tea until such time as my services were required. The street outside was empty. The midday sun had sent people scurrying under pub parasols and into the surrounding parks. Hat sales that day were not at their best.

I had invested in a rather nice range of straw hats and offered a bespoke service to personalise them. This seemed to do well at first but the heat dulls the creative mind and people simply don't want to have to think in this weather. As a result - I was left with a box of very nice but very plain straw hats and several plastic bags of assorted ribbons, bows, flowers and pins. Delilah had suggested eBay but I refuse to partake in such madness. I may have to swallow my pride though as dead stock is dead weight.

As I read the paper it rustled in the breeze of the fan. I was reviewing an article reporting the death of Peter Kürbis. It was a small article, given the significance of the event on our humble allotments. It detailed the victim's name, age and address. The reference to the use of a vegetable as a murder weapon was very matter-of-fact; never mind that it would have taken enormous force to kill someone with a pumpkin. We were clearly dealing with a very determined and dangerous individual when it came to our murderer.

It went on to say little more than *'the police are pursuing several lines of enquiry'*. Of course, they requested that anyone with any information should come forward. Naturally, I had relayed all I knew of Peter Kürbis and his antics at the time of my interview and the allotment trampling on Saturday.

With my mind back on the allotment murder I began to think once more about the characters in our little tale, in particular one Derek Nyeman. Could he really be our murderer?

I have already mentioned the infamous rosebay willowherb that floats its feathery seeds from Mrs Devine's allotment to my own, but a second curse is goosegrass. Dennis Nyeman, is very much akin to goosegrass; his presence on the plots is an anathema. The hooked leaves of goosegrass creep along the ground clinging to and suffocating any other plants that dare to grow in its path. Perhaps, like goosegrass, it was in Nyeman's nature to destroy whatever was in his.

It was then that I remembered something about Saturday morning that I had, until now, not registered.

In the far corner of the allotments is a car park. Living but half a mile up the road, I of course walk to the allotments and enter from the opposite side to the car park. As I said before there are fifty plots in total and it is impossible to see all the plots from mine; however, I do like to know who's there.

Who knows when you might be ambushed by a *'friendly'* neighbour asking how your daughter is, or how you're coping on your own these days. It's been nearly ten years since my wife passed away, and yet the women of Tuesbury still find it difficult to believe that I cope very well, thank you. The car park, therefore, often provides a good indicator as to who is on the allotment and any unwanted casseroles that may come my way.

At the hour I had arrived on Saturday, the car park would normally be empty. But as I replayed the events of Saturday morning in my mind, I recalled a very familiar, gold-coloured, 1960s Renault van. The very same van that is driven by Dennis Nyeman. Given his vehement passion for walking, the irony is not lost on me.

It is a well-known fact that a criminal cannot resist re-visiting the scene of his crime. The van was clear evidence that Nyeman had been present on the allotment that morning. Was he returning to the scene of his crime? Usually his favoured time was the school run as this was when he had the biggest audience, so why would he choose six a.m. on Saturday morning?

Delilah was possibly correct. Maybe Nyeman had finally cracked.

I was deep in thought, gazing out of the window, not really looking at anything, when I became aware of two suited gentlemen approaching from the other side of the street. To quote Noël Coward *"Only mad dogs and Englishmen go out in the midday sun"* and since most Englishmen were hiding in establishments that offered refreshments, exactly what kind of mad dogs were these?

The taller gentleman was a step or two in front of his companion. He wore a crisp black suit and white shirt, his collar was undone and he was missing a tie. His dark hair was styled into a very modern quiff and his clean-shaven face frowned in the bright light of the sun. He was clearly a chap who looked after his appearance and was probably a familiar face at the local gym.

They approached the door and entered with an air of supreme confidence.

'Good afternoon sir', the taller gentleman said as he fished around in his jacket pocket, 'I wondered if I might speak to a Mr Hetherington.' He finished rummaging and produced a warrant card as identification. I studied the card; this was Detective Sergeant Claringdon of the Metropolitan Police. His colleague was Detective Constable Alston, also proffered a warrant card.

Closing the paper I answered, 'I am Mr Hetherington.'

'We wondered if we could ask you a few questions about Mrs Devine?'

'Of course,' I replied, assuming they were investigating the link between Mrs Devine and the victim, Mr Kürbis.

'Is this a convenient moment sir?' Sergeant Claringdon asked.

'Of course,' I reiterated, 'not a problem. I will turn the sign.' I said indicating the door to the shop. 'And can I offer you a drink? I have some iced tea, which is most refreshing in this heat.'

Perhaps annoyed by what could be considered irreverent conversation, in the circumstances, the officers were curt in their refusal of refreshment. I turned the sign, as I had suggested, before we went through to the back of the shop where I have a small office.

Pushing my ledgers to one side, the sergeant perched on the desk whilst his colleague loitered in the doorway, leaning on the door jamb. I took advantage of the empty seat at the desk and the conversation began.

'I understand you own the allotment next to Mrs Samphire Devine, Mr Hetherington, is this correct?'

'Yes' I replied, reluctant to elaborate just yet.

'And how do you know Mrs Devine?'

'I don't know her well. She lives in the same village as me and that's about it sergeant'.

'Could you tell us a little about your relationship with Mrs Devine?'

'Apart from the rosebay willowherb that drifts across from her allotment to mine, I would not say we had any kind of relationship at all!' I smiled.

'If we could just stick to the relevant facts please sir.' Said Sergeant Claringdon.

Not sure as to where this line of questioning was going, I decided it was my turn to ask a question.

'I take it this is about the murder?' I said.

'We are aware of the recent events on your allotment sir but I'm here with regards to the whereabouts of Reuben Devine.'

'Well, I'm not sure how I can help you with that gentleman. Suffice to say I thought he was behind bars.' I replied.

'I'm afraid not sir. Mr Devine was recently moved to an open prison to serve the last few months of his sentence. He has not returned to the prison for two days.'

My face must have said it all, because his colleague shifted in the doorway and coughed. So Reuben Devine was missing! I'd always thought open prison relied too heavily on the integrity of its residents.

'And how am I to help you with this?' I said, after an awkward silence.

'Perhaps Mrs Devine has said something that may be of use in relocating him, sir. Or maybe you've even seen Mr Devine at the allotments.'

'I'm not sure I follow you sergeant. I have already said I know little about Mrs Devine and I'm quite sure if I'd seen Mr Devine on the allotments recently, I would have informed the police immediately!' I looked him square in the eyes.

'Mr Devine was an acquaintance of Jay Cartwright. A name I believe you are familiar with.'

My smiled waned. Taking a deep breath in to control my despair with the sergeant, I replied.

'He shot me in the foot sergeant, whilst I was trying to apprehend him. I fail to see how exactly that links me to the exploits of Reuben Devine or indeed his wife? I do not make a habit of fraternising with criminals!'

'Well, sir it does seem a little odd that your name crops up in relation to both the Devines and Mr Cartwright.'

The sergeant's attitude was finally beginning to irritate me. His insidious implications and demands for information were verging on impertinent. I do not care for impertinence.

There was a long silence as I decided what to do next. Maybe it was the arrogance of youth or maybe our dear sergeant was slightly delusional. He was interrogating a man in his sixties, with a limp and a cane, in a hat shop; hardly a master criminal. As I have said earlier, I do not wish to criticise our police force, after all they are only doing their best, but this man was clearly an idiot.

'I don't think I can help you any further, gentlemen.' I stood up from the chair. I was well aware of my rights and delusional or not, this was beginning to sound a little too much like a stitch-up. 'I'll be happy to answer any further questions in the presence of my solicitor.'

Constable Alston moved from the door as I left the office and walked back into the shop towards the front door.

'I don't think that will be necessary sir, we'll be in touch', the sergeant said as he walked past me and through the open door.

The constable paused in the doorway and smiled, cringing at his superior's brash confidence. 'Sorry to have bothered you Mr Hetherington.'

'By the way,' I added, 'you might want to talk to Derek Nyeman. I remembered I'd seen his van in the allotment car park very early on Saturday morning; a most unusual hour for him. It might be worth investigating.' I smiled at the uncomfortable detective.

'Thank you Mr Hetherington.' He said.

'Come on Alston'. Sergeant Claringdon shouted from halfway across the road.

As the door closed and the bell jangled behind Alston. I did not flip the sign back; instead I locked the door. This was just ludicrous! Me, an acquaintance of Jay Cartwright! Had the sergeant read none of the notes pertaining to that case? I needed another espresso.

I used the shop phone in the back office to ring Delilah. Not wanting to discuss the accusations over the phone, I asked her to meet me at Frascati, when she'd finished work. She was currently working on a dig in Deerton, about a mile from Tuesbury, so I knew it wouldn't be too far out of her way. I needed to know if our detectives had been to see her. If I was in the frame then you can bet Delilah was too.

The Grapevine:

Both the Greeks and the Romans worshipped the god of the grapevine. To the Greeks he was Dionysus and to the Romans he was Bacchus, but to both cultures he represented wine, entertainment, ecstasy and excess.

Claringdon did indeed question Delilah, but before I continue I'd like to share with you some of my diary entries. The next ten days were to yield little new information, or at least that is how it appeared at the time. I am not a compulsive diary writer and my entries are sporadic but now, looking back at the conversations and events of those few days, perhaps they were not as fruitless as I at first thought. So here are the entries for your consideration, and, as you will surely see, it is not always the extraordinary that provides the solution to the mystery but often the very ordinary.

Thursday 2nd October

The allotment is flourishing once more. The sweet corn is reaching for the sky and the pumpkins are swelling with the October rain showers. Some of the chard and beetroot, spared from the forensic onslaught last week, are making tremendous autumnal salads. They complement the pork chops from Rawlinson's butchers perfectly. Eleanor would have loved them. She was always a fan of raw beetroot.

To fill in some of the sparser patches left by the magnum boots of the officers, Delilah has planted some flowers in containers using an idea she saw in a gardening magazine.

In the raised bed I've started off the onions and garlic sets. I've gone for Troy, Yellow Moon, Red Baron and Vellelado Wight.

I am also pleased to report that a couple of the radishes have rallied and may well grow to be very good competition entries for the Autumn Show.

Friday 3rd October

A most intriguing obituary revealed itself to me this morning whilst I was drinking my ten o' clock coffee, which leaves me with an interesting prospect. On page twenty-two of the Tuesbury Observer there appeared the following:

'Matilda Corrina Devine, aged 84, of Tuesbury, passed away peacefully on Wednesday, 1st October 2013, at Wisteria House Care Home, Compton.

Matilda was a much-loved resident of Compton, where she lived, since leaving her childhood home in Tuesbury, at the age of 61. A widow, Mrs Devine, was a sister to Michael, mother to Porche and Rueben, and grandmother to four. She will be sadly missed by her family and many friends.

The funeral service will be held on the Saturday 18th October at 11AM at St Mary's Church, Tuesbury.'

It is too much of a coincidence for the Reuben mentioned in this announcement not to be the Reuben Devine currently on the run.

So, will Reuben risk his freedom and make an appearance at his mother's funeral, I ask myself? Surely, he could not be so heartless as to miss saying goodbye to his mother? It could be that he has already said his goodbyes but, as Matilda reportedly lived in a care home, how are we to suppose he did so without attracting considerable attention?

And so we must wait for the eighteenth and the possibility that Reuben Devine will reveal himself.

Saturday 4th October

Today I must gather my thoughts. This morning the shop had a distinct lack of trade. There is a definite lull in customers as I wait for the Christmas rush to get going.

It has provided me with the time to look through some old newspaper articles that I photocopied in the library.

My visit from Detectives Claringdon and Alston at the beginning of the week has piqued my interest in Reuben Devine. So I have turned to the newspapers to shed some light on the whole affair, not always advisable. Nevertheless, I have decided to make a note of what I have found:

Facts in regards to Devine's Diablos

> *– Bogus security firm always overpriced so they never got the job but were able to scope out the property layout.*
> *– Always large houses.*
> *– Properties targeted were in London, Hertfordshire, Buckinghamshire and Surrey.*
> *– Only Devine and one other was caught. Others involved but honour among thieves prevailed and they were not given up.*
> *– Not all items stolen were retrieved.*

— Investigation open ended as victims' property left unreturned and members of the gang not found.

How does this relate to Peter Kürbis?

— The Devines own the allotment next to mine and therefore close to Kürbis.

— Were the rumours true? Was Samphire Devine conducting an affair with Peter Kürbis?

— Did Reuben Devine find out?

Questions:

— Who were the other members of the gang?

— With an organised criminal like Devine on the loose, would he risk murder?

— With members of the gang still at large, does Reuben have someone on the outside helping him?

Monday 6th October

The pumpkins are ripening nicely and the foliage is starting to die down. Unfortunately, none of my pumpkins will make the grade after the disaster that befell them last month but Delilah's may make it yet and she continues to give them the attention they need. The stems are starting to crack and next week we must pick them and place them in the greenhouse for curing ready for the show on the fifteenth.

The last of the Borlotti beans have now dried and I spent most of the morning gathering them from their brittle pods. Once soaked, they will make excellent additions to winter stews.

I have ordered some green manure seeds to grow in the empty ground over winter - grazing rye, as I'm planting a little late this year.

Tuesday 7ᵗʰ October

Delilah has been very excitable today. The dig she is working on has uncovered an old Roman mosaic. It depicts the image of Bacchus, suggesting the villa they are excavating was important in its time.

All Delilah's talk of Bacchus brings me back to the question: does Reuben Devine have a man on the outside? If some of Reuben Devine's gang remains at large in the community then he *must* have someone on the 'outside' that may help him. Could this have been Peter Kürbis?

Perhaps the fun-loving Kürbis, heart and soul of the party with his love of the grape was our very own Bacchus of Tuesbury. Possibly, through his partying he drew too much attention to himself. I have no idea what he did for a living and he must have got his money from somewhere. Could it have been the spoils of crime?

I shared my thoughts and findings with Delilah and Ed whilst in the café today. Delilah is sure that she recognises the address of one of the properties Devine's Diablos burgled and is going to look through her address book later this evening. Delilah is also suggesting she visit Cartwright in prison to discover more but I am immovable on this subject.

Ed made an interesting contribution, suggesting that perhaps Samphire and Peter were in fact planning to run away together with Devine's criminal proceeds. Gossip, of course, with no solid facts but possibly worth considering. Peter Kürbis is definitely mixed up in this somehow but was he just a hapless pawn that Samphire was toying with, or was he indeed up to his neck in it?

The whole conversation seemed to leave us, yet again, with more questions than answers.

Friday 10th October

A mug of herbal tea with Mary this evening proved a most enjoyable distraction. In the cool of the evening her homemade blackberry tea is warming and it felt good to rest my legs a little after turning over the soil ready to plant the green manure.

She is unsettled by the murder of Peter Kürbis and has made an addition of Cedar branches above the front door of her already eclectically decorated caravan. Apparently, Cedar wards off the evil spirits, for which she blames the murder. I gently suggested that the perpetrator was altogether more human; however, she would not have it and muttered some old saying about rooks and death. On this point, I was inclined to agree.

Quite contrary to the evil spirits, she was then keen to discuss with me, who I thought might have put an end to our fellow allotment owner. She was also keen to recount tales of the siren, as she called her, Samphire Devine. In shifting the blame from the rooks to Mrs Devine could it be that she believes the malevolent spirit resides within a human after all.

My replies were a little lacklustre due to my frustration at the dead ends this case is providing. She suggested I needed Vervain to boost the energy within my chakras. I've never heard such rot but I would never be so crass as to say that to Mary. She's a loveable eccentric and indeed time creates eccentricity in us all.

I concede I do find Mary's blackberry tea very relaxing and Delilah tells me she has been suffering from insomnia recently; very unlike her. So when we were in Frascati earlier this evening, I recommended the tea for its sleep inducing qualities. Delilah seemed quite interested so I've promised to get the recipe from Mary when I next see her.

Chakras aside, Mary's herbal tea recipes are really rather good. She gave me a lovely recipe for the lavender lemon honey that she uses in our tea instead of sugar. It might be rather pleasant in iced tea too. If only I'd had it during the heat of September.

Looking back on these diary entries, I am forced to confront my own stupidity. So many people intrigued by the death of a seemingly simple fellow, who did nothing more than enjoy his drink, parties and women. It could be said that people often gossip when they have nothing better to do but sometimes it pays to examine the motivation for that gossip a little more closely. All too often the answer is too close to be seen.

The Bramble

Michaelmas is the feast of the archangel
Michael and, in days gone by has been celebrated
on the eleventh of October. Legend tells that on
this day the devil was banished from heaven. So, on
Michaelmas, the devil spits on boughs of
blackberries rendering them unfit to eat.

Despite those initially fruitless days of October, some enlightenment came unexpectedly from Sergeant Claringdon. He had questioned Delilah the day after visiting the shop. But, as they say, forewarned is forearmed and she reacted to his questions in a very different manner to mine. A manner that was more useful.

It appears there is something alluring about a woman covered in mud, holding a bone brush and professing her dislike for criminals. The result was that Sergeant Claringdon bought Miss Delibes lunch at a local bistro in Deerton. Delilah was able to use her womanly wiles to glean an alarming amount of information from the detective.

Over lunch, Claringdon told Delilah that Reuben Devine had just two months of his eleven-year sentence to serve, when he was moved to an open prison. During his preceding stay in Wandsworth prison, he had become acquainted with Jay Cartwright. Three weeks ago he failed to check in at Coldarth. The police were looking for him, not only in connection with the murder of Peter Kürbis but also in connection with a spate of burglaries, some of which had occurred before Devine's escape. His disappearance had not been reported in the papers as it was felt he was not a danger to the community and the police did not wish to cause unnecessary alarm.

No doubt sensing weakness, Delilah went on to ask about the burglaries and learned that the criminals involved had used a similar modus operandi to Devine's Diablos. Ostensibly, the police thought Devine had someone on the outside. This was as I had suspected, however, I had not been aware of the most recent burglaries. They had not shown up in my newspaper searches.

She had dared further to ask if the murderer had been caught on camera? Delilah then discovered that the cameras on the allotments were all dummies, except for one. That was the camera on Mrs Devine's shed, which I admit had escaped my attention entirely. Attached to the side of the shed its presence was shielded from my allotment by a large buddleia.

Unfortunately the camera only focused on the door of the shed and provided no information as to the comings and goings on my allotment. I'm not convinced Claringdon should have revealed this fact to Miss Delibes. He was most informative.

Perhaps his judgment was impaired. Delilah can be difficult to resist when she wants something, or perhaps it was an attempt to gain information through fair exchange; Claringdon's investigative skills are *surely* beyond me. Either way when Delilah declined his invitation to dinner, she'd found him a little less amenable. She was unable to mine any more information from him. I was, however, astounded at the information she had managed to obtain from the pompous detective.

October arrived and with it Michaelmas. As you have seen almost a fortnight had now passed in my diary. My trips to the library to collect newspaper clippings, and the community's desire to gossip about Peter's demise, added nothing to our investigation.

Delilah had, however, traced the address she had recognised and found that there was a reason for its familiarity. It was the country home of one of her old lecturers at Cambridge, Professor Malus and she had wasted no time in arranging to meet him a week later. The meeting is this evening.

So, there we were, ten days later and no further forward. Reuben Devine was still on the loose, Samphire Devine had not been seen on the allotments since the demise of Peter Kürbis and I had not received a penny of compensation for the damage to my allotment. I was thankful that a stern letter from my solicitor, mentioning police harassment, had subdued any further enquires into my assumed involvement from the Metropolitan Police.

Everything was quiet until the morning of October the eleventh.

The sun still shone, though thankfully not as hot, and now the sunshine was interspersed with rain, making watering the allotment a less frequent task. My sweet corn had recovered and I'm pleased to say even the pumpkins had rallied.

The rooks had not returned but the village had definitely seen an increase in crows and magpies in their absence. On the way to the allotment that morning my thoughts had been interrupted by the squawking of a crow on the thatched roof of a cottage on the High Street. As the saying goes, '*A crow on the thatch, soon death lifts the latch*'. I now know this was an omen.

When I arrived at the gate to the allotments, I could see Mary, sitting outside her caravan enjoying the first of the morning's rays. Her shawl was pulled tight around her and she was wearing her usual diklo scarf. The scarf was pulled forward, hiding her face. There were none of the usual smells emanating from the caravan. The curtains were drawn and the ramshackle greenhouse door was wide open. The drawn curtains were not unusual; Mary was a very private woman. The open greenhouse door was. Aloe veras need protection from the cold night air and an early October morning can be just as cold, as indeed this one was. I waved, but I assumed the scarf prevented her from seeing me.

A few yards on and I reached my own allotment where the pumpkins once again demanded my attention and I thought no more of the open door. I began to hoe around our prize gourds, enjoying the fresh cool air of the morning. Of the five pumpkins left, two were Delilah's. They were the only real contenders for the show. Later today we would pick them and leave them to cure in the greenhouse. I finished up with the hoe and attached the hose to the water butt.

Glancing over at Mary's plot, I could just see her through the shrubs of her allotment. She was still seated in the very same position; hunched over. Perhaps she had fallen asleep? It was still early after all.

The water from the hose splashed my gardening boots with mud as it rebounded off the soil and I was forced to concentrate once more on my gardening; endeavouring to avoid spraying the skins of pumpkins. Any sun would burn through the water droplets and create ugly marks that would not impress the judges. I finished and coiled up the hose, hanging it on the side of the shed. Locking up the tools again, I walked down the path out of the allotments. I had just enough time to go home and get changed, ready for another day in the shop.

Perhaps it was instinct, the fact she hadn't waved, or the greenhouse door that bothered me. Something made me turn back before reaching the gate once more. Instead, I headed for Mary's wild allotment where she still sat in the chair.

As you might expect, Ms Ananassa only grows what you might call medicinal or herbal plants on her plot. Over the years I have known her, she has taught me much about these plants. As I walked up the little path between the shrubs I could smell the sweet scent of blackberries rotting on their boughs. The pink flowers of *Rubus ulmifolius* had long gone. Only its long curved thorns remained.

I abstained from fresh blackberries as a general rule. The seeds often wedge in my teeth and are the cause of great annoyance, so I simply don't eat them. Delilah tells me that archaeologists can tell the difference between a raspberry and a blackberry seed. I can see why, given their persistence in taking up residence in one's teeth. Archaeologists are probably very familiar with them. It is no wonder Roman centurions were so aggressive. Heavy armour, battle-hungry leaders, and then a dastardly blackberry seed wedges itself in your back molar.

A nettle patch grabbed at my ankles and I yelped as one of them stung me. Mary did not move. I could see that her chin was resting on her chest and her hand held a mug limply. A teapot and strainer occupied the little table in front of her.

She looked to be sleeping peacefully in an old wooden rocking chair. Her dark hair was always covered with a diklo scarf and only the odd stray wisp around her face gave away the colour. Wearing a long skirt, shawl and high neck blouse, she was always dressed older than her years. The smells that wafted from the caravan created a dichotomy of image when joined by the angelic voice that often mingled with the little puffs of steam that rose from the chimney.

I had now reached the wintergreens that bordered the end of the allotment. I was within two feet of the sleeping Romany. Surely she must have heard me approaching. Thanks to the nettles, I'd made enough noise. I really was beginning to wonder what on earth I was doing there. Despite our frequent evening communes for tea on the terrace, I felt like an intruder. But here I was and here she was, distinctly unresponsive. The whole thing made me very uneasy.

I announced my presence with a friendly *'good morning'* but she did not stir. I'd come this far and I felt a little silly turning back so I reached out to touch her shoulder. As I did, the mug slipped from her hand, rolled off her lap and landed on the hard standing where it smashed into several pieces. I'm sure you know what's coming next, for I felt compelled to reach once more for the carotid artery and any possible signs of life. There were none.

I looked across to the car park and could see no other cars. Here I was on my own, with another dead body. It was then, and only then, it occurred to me that finding another corpse, in such close proximity to my own allotment, really did not look good for me. There was only one thing I could do in this situation and that was ring the police. Using my own mobile phone, my only concession to modern technology, I made the call. I then stayed exactly where I was and did not touch anything else until the police arrived.

I don't mind telling you that waiting on your own at the edge of a misty allotment with a dead body is not a pleasurable experience and one I hope never to have to repeat. I swear I saw Ms Ananassa move on a couple of occasions: a slight rise and fall of the chest, a twitch of the hand. Most unnerving.

Two uniformed constables arrived first. I was advised to step to one side and wait for the arrival of their colleagues. I was not to go anywhere. I pointed out the smashed cup and suggested that it might be vital evidence. The officers did not take kindly to my input and so I waited patiently on the path between the allotments. I felt sure this was our murderer again. The discovery of two dead bodies within a month of each other had definitely put me on edge. Finally, a black Mercedes joined the first police car in the car park.

The arrival of a Detective Inspector Knighton, accompanied by Claringdon did nothing to improve my morning. Claringdon's statement of, '*Well, well, well Mr Hetherington fancy seeing you here,*' was loaded with implication, which, at that moment, I could not refute.

Thankfully, Delilah also appeared about half an hour after the police. Miss Delibes has an alarming knack of turning up just when she's needed. She calls it women's intuition. I think it's more likely to be a homing instinct for gossip, nevertheless, she had seen the police cars at the allotment on her way to the dig. Her arrival did soften Claringdon's attitude somewhat. It did not prevent a further implication that Delilah and I were somehow in cahoots. An outrageous slur on both our characters and one that Delilah dismissed with competent dignity.

'Sergeant Claringdon, Mr Hetherington is a very good friend of mine, definitely not the sort of man to run around committing murder. I suggest you desist with this line of inquiry before I am forced to take this up with your superiors', she said.

After making her position clear with regards to the implication that she herself was involved, she had given him a look of such indignation that the sergeant had in fact blushed. Something that I am not at all sure he is used to.

I felt it best not to answer any further questions until I once more had the advice of my solicitor. So I was asked to accompany the detectives down to the police station. I obliged, as poor Mary's allotment was starting to gather a crowd. Delilah eventually made her way to work but not before giving Sergeant Claringdon several more accusatory looks and insisting that I ring her as soon I was home again.

Whilst I was waiting for my solicitor in the interview room, I considered the events of the last few weeks. How had I managed to get myself mixed up in another murder?

After our escapades last year, Delilah and I had laughed at the idea of forming a detective agency in her mother's old art gallery. Instead, she had set up a little museum to teach school children about artefacts from her digs. In hindsight, it may have been better to set up as private investigators!

I began to wonder, as Delilah had, if Nyeman did have anything to do with this. The ancient right-of-way, for which he was campaigning, also passed through Mary Anassasa's allotment. I still found it hard to imagine him capable of murder. An egomaniac yes, but a murderer? No.

Then there was the case of Reuben Devine's disappearance, coupled with the absence of his wife from the allotments. According to rumour (Delilah is an incorrigible gossip), Mrs Devine was heartbroken at the death of Peter Kürbis. This was the reason for her unavailability. But Mrs Devine must know that her husband was on the loose. Surely this was a more likely to cause her to lie low. If they had any sense the police would have put Mrs Devine under surveillance of some kind, and not wasted their time interviewing me.

The burglaries were also of interest; although how they connected to the murders I was not yet sure. Delilah was still offering to use one of the visiting orders Jay persistently sent her, despite her ignoring them. But again I made my thoughts very clear on this matter. She was not to visit that man ever, especially as it may incriminate her further, giving Claringdon more ammunition.

Finally, if, in fact, her death was anything to do with Peter's murder, I had to question how an introvert such as Mary had become involved? The last time we'd spoken was the day we drank blackberry tea and discussed the value of Vervain, Cedar, evil spirits and our absent friends the rooks. Had she been trying to tell me something?

Sitting in the interview room, it occurred to me that it was still unclear whether or not Mary had been murdered! It was only my gut feeling that led me to this assumption. It is possible she had a congenital condition that caused her to shuffle off. Maybe she muddled up her herbal teas. This last thought made me swallow hard.

How Claringdon could assume anything at this point I did not know, but I wasn't taking any risks. If they wanted to question me, it would be in the presence of my solicitor. Clearly the death of Peter Kürbis had just been the start. And at this rate, I wasn't getting many hats sold.

The Fig Tree

The Greeks believed that the God Saturn
discovered the fruit of the fig tree. In Roman
legend, the basket carrying the twins Romulus and
Remus is caught up on the roots of a fig tree,
securing their rescue by the she-wolf Lupa. During
the eighteenth century, it was considered the tree
of choice for wealthy, eccentric Englishmen and
deeply mistrusted by the common man. Now the
tree has come to symbolise knowledge and
wisdom. For Buddhists it is thought that Buddha
himself achieved enlightenment whilst sitting
beneath the boughs of a fig tree.

The rain beat down on the green, white and red
awning of Frascati. Rivulets of water scurried along the
gutters and the storm drains bubbled in delight. It had
been several months since we'd had what you might call
a decent drop of rain and now it came; relentless,
soaking you to the bone if you dared to step outside.
Watching it from the safety of the cafe was a delight. I
have always been fond of thunderstorms. The
pumpkins were safely tucked away in the greenhouse,
ready for the show, so any damage on the allotment was
collateral, rather than significant.

It was nine o' clock, not early by my standards, but it
seemed it was only I who had ventured out into the
glory of the storm to patronise the little café. Of course
Ed had been there since the early hours, making dough
for his famous calzone. Frascati is only closed on
Mondays. Ed's life is the café, his family's pride and joy.
On the rare occasion he is not there he can be found at
the Badgers' Holt or the greyhound races at Meriton
Park.

Delilah's dig had been postponed for the day when they saw the weather forecast and I had arranged to meet her at Frascati at nine thirty. She was to tell me about her meeting with her old Professor. I never like to be late and so I occupied myself by reading the paper whilst I waited for her to arrive.

The rain drummed on the café's canopy and I warmed my damp hands on a mug of filter coffee. My table was beside the kitchen door, at the front of the café. I was sitting facing the road and this was my favourite spot. I could observe the world outside, and the smells from the kitchen were comforting. I could hear the methodical thump and phut of the pizza dough as it took its beating from Ed. The wind pushed more rain under the awning and it ran down the large front windows, pixelating my view of the High Street.

I turned back to the paper, open on the table in front of me. There was already a report on Mary's death. The police concluded it was natural causes. They must have rushed the post-mortem and, considering the circumstances, I'm not surprised.

Consequently, I had heard nothing more from Claringdon. He'd had little to question me about yesterday. An hour and a half I'd waited for my solicitor. One wonders what one is paying such an exorbitant amount per hour for. Half my day was wasted waiting for him to arrive and then for him to tell me what I already knew- *your connection to the victims is purely circumstantial*. Still I was glad he was there. With a solicitor present it gave me peace of mind to know that Claringdon couldn't get away with any more of his outrageous accusations.

Sergeant Claringdon was, however, interested in the nature of Mary's caravan and wanted to know if she lived there permanently. I'd never really thought about this before. I'd assumed she did, but I suppose the legality of such an abode was debatable. I'm sure that Nyeman would have known this too. Maybe he was the evil spirit to which Mary referred. Perhaps he had found a way to get her caravan, and home, removed from the allotments. As I said to Claringdon yesterday, I hardly felt it was relevant any more, as Mary certainly wasn't living there now.

I remained unconvinced that Mary's death was a simple medical matter. It is true that when she took her herbal tea on an evening, she also took several tablets with it. I never knew what these pills were and would never have had the impertinence to ask. What bothered me was Mary was a woman in her forties, not sixties. She appeared to be the picture of health. I assumed the pills were some of her own making, perhaps Bloodroot for healing strength or Valerian to help her sleep, or some such nonsense.

The comical sight of Delilah, trying to dodge the raindrops, as she raced across the road, interrupted my thoughts. Above her head she held a woefully inadequate plastic A4 folder and instead of protecting her from the rain, water ran off it and onto her jeans. Her flip-flops flicked water from the puddles up the back of her legs and by the time she had reached the safety of Frascati, she was soaked through.

As she opened the door a gust of wind blew more rain in with her.

'You know what they say' she chirped, 'in the words of Crowded House, always take the weather with you.'

She shook herself off on the mat and it was then that I noticed Bertie was with her. The little dog looked nonplussed and for a moment the two of them stood in unison shaking the rain off their coats. Recently Ed had turned a blind eye to Delilah's Jack Russell, Bertie. He'd even removed the 'NO DOGS' sign from the front door. I have to admit Bertie was always very well behaved. He would curl up under the table to dream of chasing cats or rabbits or whatever it is that dogs dream about. Occasionally, he'd wake to receive the odd titbit from the table, another habit of Delilah's of which, I did not approve.

She approached the table, grinning in spite of her bedraggled appearance. Her jeans bore a tidemark half way up her shins. Rat-tails of hair stuck to her face. She pushed back them behind her ear and wiped the water from her nose. Her thin pac-a-mac clung to her clothes and continued to drip on the hard resin surface of the café floor. She peeled if off, sticking it to the coat stand, by the door and Ed appeared with a mop and bucket, muttering something about health and safety.

She slapped the wet plastic folder down on the table, spraying water over the tablecloth and my now dry hands. Apologising, she grabbed a handful of napkins, patted the table dry, and began.

'Sorry Blake, I'm just so excited. We might actually have a breakthrough here! Bertie, lie down.' She thumped down in the chair and wedged the soaking napkins in between a vase and a menu. Bertie disappeared under the table to take up his position. A breakthrough indeed! Well we needed one. I could see she was bursting to tell me all about her meeting with Professor Malus and I was more than happy to listen. The storm rumbled on outside and the coat stand dripped in time with the ticking clock.

Ferreting around in the folder, Delilah retrieved a scruffy bit of paper with a spider diagram on it. In the middle, encompassed in a pink spiky oval shape, was the name PETER KÜRBIS - a pretty good starting point. Leading off from that were squares with more names and plot numbers, presumably from the allotment. She handed me the diagram and started to tell me about her meeting.

Devine's Diablos had broken into Professor Malus' house, twelve years ago. Way before Delilah had met him at Cambridge. Professor Malus was an avid and eclectic collector of artefacts and antiques. The sheer volume of his collection meant he had not made a note of all the items in his possession. Delilah described to me a house full of dig finds, first edition novels and Clarice Cliff pottery.

Professor Malus had become agitated when Delilah had mentioned the murder and advised her not to go *'raking around in the past'*. This had simply made Delilah even more determined. Laughing at the idea of an archaeologist not *'raking around in the past'*, she pressed the professor for more information but he would not be drawn on the subject. Delilah went on to talk enthusiastically about the different items Professor Malus had collected over the last twelve years to replace the burgled items.

'Where's Mary?' I interrupted. I had become distracted by the diagram, an unfortunate habit of mine, and had noticed that in the little squares surrounding Peter Kürbis, there was no Mary Ananassa.

'What?' Delilah stopped in the midst of describing a Grecian vase with a very Grecian scene on it.

'Where's Mary?' I repeated.

'Oh Blake, you're not listening, this is important,' she said and tutted. Ed appeared from the kitchen minus the mop and bucket. He placed a Vesuvius of cappuccino in front of Delilah. The cup could barely contain the froth. How Delilah could not see Ed's infatuation was beyond me.

'Oooh, have you solved the mystery?' Ed said, his eyebrows rose above eager eyes. He pulled a chair up and sat at the table with us.

'Well I think we've had a breakthrough, but Blake's not listening.'

'Sorry', I sighed, there really was no other reply to this. Leaning forward, I placed the diagram on the table and waited for Delilah to continue. Mary's absence from the chart would have to wait.

'Well, although Professor Malus was reluctant to talk to me about the burglary, he did want to talk to me about my little museum and the dangers of buying artefacts on the black market. I obviously reassured him that this was not something that I did and that the finds in the museum were all given to me from the dig sites I worked on.' She hesitated. 'But I have a theory.'

'Go on', Ed encouraged.

'I've been reading those newspaper articles,' she said tapping the folder on the table, 'and they got me thinking. Professor Malus didn't catalogue all the items he collected. So, first of all, how do the police know if they recovered them all, and secondly, maybe it wasn't just the quantity that stopped the Professor from recording all his treasures?'

'I see.' I replied starting to understand where Delilah was going with this one. 'What if one of the items missing was a *black market* item?'

'Exactly!' Delilah said hitting the table. Bertie jumped and whimpered. For a moment Delilah disappeared under the table to soothe her little hound.

'Brilliant!' Ed exclaimed. 'But what's that got to do with Peter?'

There was a pause in the conversation and I took the opportunity to look back at the diagram.

Delilah reappeared and replied, 'I'm not sure yet.' I saw her giving Ed a sideways glance. She only ever looked that coy when she was up to something. Delilah knew all right and so did I.

If there was an item missing from the burglary carried out by Devine's Diablos all those years ago, then perhaps it was an artefact that Professor Malus had bought on the black market. He'd therefore, be unable to report it missing. If this was the case, perhaps Peter and Samphire knew about it? Could it be an item of considerable value and, therefore, worth murdering for? Unfortunately, suppositions were going to get us nowhere. It was a breakthrough, but only a theoretical one.

Delilah had changed the subject and was now telling Ed about the mosaic they had unearthed at the dig. He was transfixed, but perhaps not by the subject matter. Bertie huffed under the table nudging my foot as he repositioned himself. With the toe of my shoe, I rubbed his tummy and he sneezed, happily content once more.

I sipped at my, now cold, coffee. I never minded cold coffee. I was frequently interrupted in the shop and well used to drinking tepid liquids. It was strong and the beans smelt ever so slightly of chocolate and almonds. I pulled a pen from my jacket pocket to make some annotations on Delilah's diagram. Mary should at least appear on it, even if her death was not considered murder. For me, it was just too much of a coincidence. Two deaths in as many weeks! Unless of course the absence of a rookery really had doomed our allotments. In which case, there was little hope, as the bell tolls for us all.

'Bacchus isn't just associated with grapes though,' I overheard Delilah say as I tuned into her enthusing once more, 'no, he was associated with figs too. Wisdom and wine, what a combination.' She laughed and Ed laughed with her.

What a combination indeed, I thought mulling over the facts. But if Peter Kürbis was our Bacchus, what was his wisdom?

The Cornucopia

*Greek Mythology tells of Zeus's foster mother,
Amalthaea and how she fed Zeus on goat's milk
when he was a child. Legend has it that one day
the horn of the goat fell off. As a gift for Zeus,
Amalthaea filled the horn with fruit and flowers.
Pleased with his gift Zeus took it and placed it in
the sky. There it became a constellation. The
Cornucopia has become the symbol of plenty and
represents the fruits of the earth.*

The waiting list for our allotments had dramatically
shortened in the space of a few days, as word got round
of 'Bloody Tuesbury'. The allotment society had voted
in favour of installing lighting and security cameras, real
ones this time, to protect their members. There was
even talk of the need for public liability insurance for
allotment owners. I have no wish to bow to the whims
of our litigious society. I will never purchase liability
insurance, so that some youth can sue me for injuring
himself whilst trying to break into my shed. I am
affronted by the idea to say the least.

The twittering continued, and by the day of the
Tuesbury Autumn Show, they'd whipped themselves up
into a frenzy. The village was buzzing with talk of
murder.

The village hall was fit to burst with patrons. Some
of them were there to see the produce, others for the
craft stalls and others to partake in the dog show. Some
were simply there out of morbid curiosity. It was fair to
say Tuesbury allotments were now notorious, and not
for the size of their pumpkins.

The trestle tables had been set up in rows
lengthways across the hall; end on, to the stage, where

the prizes for fruit and veg categories would be announced later. A cornucopia of produce adorned them in a fountain of colour and smell. For me you can't beat the smell of fresh vegetables. Apart from the allotments, one of my favourite places in Tuesbury is the greengrocer on Huckspeth Road.

The categories this year included hanging baskets, floral displays, an array of seasonal fruit and vegetables, quilts, cakes and photography. As the villagers milled around the hall they passed comment on the size of Old Gratwick's giant Butternut squash, Jemima Cardon's amazing cabbage sculptures and, I'm pleased to say the magnificence of Delilah's Hundredweight pumpkins. The judges had now retired to the back office and were preparing for the award ceremony that was now only an hour away.

The show had started at two o' clock, and I'd taken the time to peruse the tables before it got too busy. I had entered a couple of categories: Sweetcorn and Radishes. I had no chance of winning with the pumpkins. Kürbis had put a stop to that. Now all hopes in that category rested on Delilah, but I tried to put thoughts of last month's devastation to the back of my mind as I walked the aisles of fruit and veg.

Bright red and purple beetroot made a wonderful display next to the rainbow chard and I have to say I was a little envious of the success of some allotment owners this year. The stony soil that makes up our plots means a great deal of cultivation is needed to get large and perfectly shaped root vegetables.

Moving on to the fruit, I was disappointed to find that some entrants had paid no attention to the rules for displaying apples. The guidelines clearly state there should be five in total displayed flower end up. This is not difficult to do, however, I was surprised to see two sets the wrong way up and one that only contained three apples. I resisted the temptation to right the wrongs of the apple display and moved on to the village homemade produce.

Medlar jam, elderflower cordial and sloe gin graced the tables this year. A new display of quilts and various crocheted items joined them and it was good to see these crafts kept alive. The gentlemen's cake display sat on a table in the middle, pride of place, between the quilts and jams. The men of Tuesbury were very proud of their ability to bake once a year.

The last trestle was entitled 'Foraging' and I became fascinated by the small baskets of wild mushrooms on offer. I wasn't entirely sure I fancied being the judge for those. The risks were pretty high; you'd have to be confident you knew your juvenile death cap from your edible puffball or straw mushroom! My fungi knowledge is limited and I wasn't at all sure of what I was looking at. I found myself peering into the baskets, hands firmly held behind my back, resisting the impulse to touch the potentially poisonous products.

Further down the table were plates of rosehips and forest fruits. The Allotment Society had made a posthumous entry for Mary Ananassa's wintergreens, which got me thinking once more about the possibilities surrounding Mary's death. Reminding me further of poor Mary, various herbal teas took their place next to chintzy teapots. Each pot was accompanied by three shot glasses of now cold tea; I assume a prerequisite for judging.

By now, I had spent a couple of hours considering the produce and lamenting my lost pumpkins, so I progressed outside to the small field adjoining the hall. Due to the predicted high turn out, the organisers had seen fit to erect a marquee on the field. It was here, on one of the plastic bucket-seated chairs, placed around the edge of the marquee, that I chose to sit. The style of the chairs reminded me of school; an enduring Robin Day design. Sitting on these seats for any length of time invoked a compulsion to fidget.

Occupying one half of the tent were yet more trestle tables but, in the other half, a small ring had been created for the dog show that was about to start. From where I sat, I had a good view of the arena, in between two rows of tables. Delilah was excited to be entering Bertie into the obedience category and was lining up at the far side of the tent with the other dog owners. Occasionally, she would bend down to scratch Bertie's ear as he watched her intently, waiting for an instruction. Or, which is far more likely, a treat of some description.

A breeze pushed under the tent sides and it wafted the smell of ripe tomatoes, onions and fresh cut grass. It reminded me of days gone by and family picnics when my daughter Jane was a child. She loved nothing better than walking to Wimbledon Common where she would hunt in the undergrowth for insects to examine under her microscope, collect flowers to press and then finally settle down to homemade bruschetta and a story read by her mother. I was becoming maudlin and so, wiping a tear from my eye, I focussed once more on the happenings in the marquee.

I was resting my foot and observing the comings and goings in the tent, when Olea Faba and her husband sat down beside me. Olea was wearing the most awful fascinator. I swear these atrocities follow me around to goad me. Cerise feathers adorning an orange headband, coupled with a lime green polyester rose, all combined to make me shudder involuntarily. The feathers fluttered in the breeze coming from the sides of the tent, causing Mrs Faba to persistently scratch her head where they tickled her hairline. Her permed hair was scraped back from her face on either side, with two plastic tortoiseshell combs to complete the ensemble.

On sitting down she leant across her husband and accosted me verbally as is often her wont. This time it was with regards to my friendship with Mary Ananassa. Unwilling to provide one of Tuesbury's most notorious dealers in jaw prattle, with anything she may consider information, I remained vague on the matter. She went on to tell me that as Mary had one traceable family member who lived in Australia. They had requested that the allotment society should clear Mary's caravan and do as they saw fit with the contents. It was the decision of the allotment society that I should be the one to do this. After all, I had been the only one to whom she ever spoke.

I began to protest; my foot did not need another allotment to dig. She insisted that I at least sort through the caravan, to ensure there was nothing of value that should not go to clearance. I acquiesced, with the agreement that should there be anything of value it would go to charity. Perhaps it was best for poor Mary if I was the one to sort through her personal possessions rather than someone who didn't know her, but the task did not fill me with joy.

After my initial conversation with Olea, she had proceeded to accost people as they passed by the chairs, engaging them in tittle-tattle. Between Mrs Faba and myself, her husband was sensibly dozing, although how he'd become comfortable enough in the chairs, I have no idea. I tried, as best I could, to ignore Olea Faba. Instead, I amused myself with the various ooohs and ahhhs, emitted by people who were looking at some rather charming miniature vegetable gardens. They had been created by the local school children and featured red currants as tomatoes. I was also observing the dog show in which Bertie seemed to be doing rather well.

There were fifteen dogs in total; a small participation by comparison to the rest of the show. The organisers seemed to have stuck to a more frivolous theme with prizes this year. There were awards for *'waggiest tail'*, *'best treat catcher'*, *'prettiest bitch'* and *'most handsome dog'*. Even the obedience category involved an array of brightly coloured tubes, a children's slide and a paddling pool. The sight of Bertie whizzing down the slide in pursuit of his treat was, in itself, a treat. It will come as no surprise that Bertie won both best treat catcher and the obedience categories. It's amazing what can be achieved with bribery.

After about twenty minutes, I became aware of the fact that Mrs Faba was actually saying something of interest to one of her associates. I don't like to eavesdrop but on occasion it has proved to be very useful. Without the benefit of eavesdropping, I may never have known the details of my late wife's social schedule, and therefore when I could surprise her with a night out to her favourite restaurant.

It was Olea's body language that alerted me to the significance of her gossiping. She had twisted in her seat, with her back to me and her arm resting on the back of the chair. She was talking to a friend from the local WI group, who was standing in the doorway of the marquee. When not scratching her head, Mrs Faba, once or twice flicked her hand in front of her nose in a dismissive fashion. The tone of her voice had dropped and I could only just hear over her husband's snoring.

'The state of that allotment, I'd be embarrassed if I were her. There's not an edible thing grown there, and that shed...'

Mrs Faba's friend nodded in agreement encouraging her to continue.

'...I've seen her go in it on a couple of occasions, but she never comes out with any tools in her hand.

Goodness knows what's in there. I've never seen her do a stroke of gardening. Such a waste. There are people with families to feed who would dearly love that plot.'

Her friend was now tutting and shaking her head.

'I made my mind up to ask her this year, what she was planting, do you know what she said?'

The friend shook her head.

' *"My fortune Olea, my fortune"*. Well, the audacity, I tell you! I've tried to be pleasant, I even offered her the excess French beans we had. I said she could come and pick them whenever she wanted. She only went and picked the broad beans and now I have hardly any dried beans to plant next year. Do you know, I don't think she has the first clue about gardening. Flouncy little upstart.'

After listening to some further mutterings about the waste of land and the scarcity of Olea's broad beans, I discovered she was, of course, referring to Samphire Devine. Some women have a way of seeking out those who are different and pecking them until they conform. However, it was undeniably interesting that Mrs Devine did not know her French beans from her broad beans; unless of course she had known exactly what she was doing.

What little I did know of Samphire though, did not lead me to believe that she was spiteful. Delilah had told me that on occasion Samphire bought Bertie a sausage sandwich if she saw them in the Badgers' Holt of an evening. In my experience, people who are kind to animals are rarely spiteful to their human counterparts.

The ringing of a bell from the dog show enclosure and the appearance of a moustached gentleman wearing a Homburg, cut Mrs Faba's conversation short. I was relieved to see someone wearing something sensible at last, even more so when I recognised it as one of my own creations. The Homburg is usually made of felt with a gutter crown and a kettle curl brim and is most definitely a gentleman's hat. The wearer was Major Turnball, a small man with a very particular appearance and the chairman of our allotment society. Standing in the centre of the ring, he announced the end of the dog show and the imminent prize giving in the village hall.

As Major Turnball finished, Samphire Devine entered the tent and sat down on the empty chair beside me. Olea Faba folded her arms and made an exaggerated eye roll, turning back in the direction of her friend. I greeted Samphire with the most benign smile I could muster. She smiled back and proceeded to rummage around in her handbag. I felt impelled to make some comment with regards to the late Mrs Devine and offered my sympathies at the sad news. Looking up from her handbag she went to reply but at that moment, Delilah appeared with Bertie.

'We really should go into the hall to see who has come first in the pumpkin competition.' And then seeing her friend; 'Are you coming Samphire?' she asked.

'Yes, I'll follow you in a minute' Samphire replied into her handbag and we left her preoccupied with her search.

Once in the hall, the crowd gathered and jostled for a position in the gaps between the rows of trestles. Major Turnball and his Homburg appeared once more and a hush fell on the hall as the all-important prizes for the fruit and vegetable categories were announced.

I have to say I phased out a little, tired by the heat created by so many bodies in such a small space. I was alerted to the proceedings with the aid of Delilah's elbow in my ribs, just in time to hear the words 'second place', 'pumpkin' and 'Faba'. A squeal pierced my eardrum as Delilah was announced in first place. She handed me Bertie's lead and used her elbows once more to fight her way to the front to collect her prize. I, of course, clapped and congratulated her. However, it was with a heavy heart, for had it not been for blasted Peter Kürbis, then I feel sure I would have been the one receiving that rosette.

I was not entirely disappointed, and I was proud to receive first prize for my Sundance sweet corn and second for my almost perfectly round Sparkler Radishes; not bad for a last minute entry.

Never one to miss an occasion, I suggested The Snicket for a celebratory dinner. Our trips there were becoming a little more infrequent due to the convenience and proximity of Frascati to the allotments, but we still find occasions to eat at our favourite restaurant.

The crowd dispersed and people started to wend their way home up the High Street. I waited by the gate for Delilah; she was revelling in the spotlight of her prize, as people congratulated her. Delilah waved her rosette in delight, at Olea Faba's back, Olea's fascinator wobbling wildly as she stomped her way across the field towards the gate. Her husband, trailing behind, was somewhat bemused by the whole affair. He had spent most of the afternoon asleep.

As I waited, I noticed Delilah stop to talk to Samphire. Their conversation was very different from the relaxed, smiling faces of Delilah's congratulators. Delilah had her hand on Samphire's crossed arms and both had their heads bowed towards one another. The conversation only lasted a couple of minutes and as Delilah removed her hand Samphire pushed her fringe out of her eyes and smiled nodding. Delilah then made her way across to the gate where I was waiting.

Later, over dinner, the wonders of a very nice Chablis and, of course, my favourite Herb Crusted Scallops, Delilah told me she had offered to accompany Samphire to her mother-in-law's funeral.

'Samphire has no idea where Reuben is, but she can't very well not go to her mother-in-law's funeral. I think she really needs a friend right now. Perhaps you should come too Blake, I'm sure you'd be welcome. Samphire's had such a bad time of it lately, it would be good to show her some support. I doubt anyone else will be there.' Delilah said and I nodded in agreement.

The possibility of attending the funeral of Matilda Devine had occurred to me, but I had no wish to intrude on the family's grief. However, Samphire wanted Delilah there and Delilah had asked me; and what better place to observe the dynamics of the Devine family. Everyone knows a funeral uncovers the truth.

The Allium

"The onion and its satin wrappings is among the most beautiful of vegetables and is the only one that represents the essence of things. It can be said to have a soul."

Charles Dudley Warner: 'My Summer in a Garden' (1871)

Friday was a long day in the shop. Perhaps the impending task, of clearing Mary's caravan, overshadowed the usual proceedings, it is hard to say. The result was that I spent the majority of my time in the back office working on a commission for six top hats. The work was for a wealthy banker whose daughter was getting married the following spring. The bands on the hats matched the bridesmaids' dresses, which were to be a very regal shade of purple.

Each hat had a small white silk cannula lily tucked into the bow on hatband. This in itself was not a challenge but on each bow the family crest was to be sewn, and my glasses had prevailed over my vanity. Holding the ribbon tight, whilst being careful not to stretch it, I worked by the light of a desk lamp with a fine size three needle and Gutermann topstitch number 968, a favourite of mine. As I worked I listened for the ting of the shop bell.

I was enjoying my task greatly and, I have to say, a large part of me resented being interrupted when, on odd occasion, the bell on the door did call for me. Whilst working on the commissions, my thoughts turned once more to the allotments. I was pleased with the progress of the new produce I'd planted in the remaining gaps. The onion sets were just starting to break the soil - I have no doubt we have the rain to thank for their speedy progress.

Alliums and their layers have long been favourites of mine. The diversity of the Allium family is what fascinates me, from the tiny spring onion or shallot to the *Allium giganteum* or giant onion. Not forgetting of course their gentle cousins of the herbaceous border, *atropurpureum* or *caeruleum*; their pom-poms of starred flowers nodding in the breeze.

When talking about a person with a complex personality, people often compare them to an onion. People have many different layers, as do onions. Mary Ananassa was just such a person.

Perhaps this is why Mary and I got on, despite our differences of opinion with regard to the application of medical science. She had layers. With this in mind, my main reservation with regard to the clearance of Mary's caravan was the uncovering of these layers and consequently her private life. Surely, she deserved to have her privacy beyond the grave.

I knew, however, that one way or another the caravan would have to be cleared, either by an impersonal clearance company or by the far too personal Olea Faba and friends. In conclusion, I decided it had better be someone who knew her. I was hardly going to get Mary's permission now. Like most unpleasant tasks in life, it simply had to be done.

The lack of sensible trade and my evening's caravan commitment encouraged me to finish up early, once again. Despite the joy I found in my work, I was painfully aware I had another less pleasurable task to fulfil; Mary's caravan was not going to clear itself. Thankfully, Delilah had kindly agreed to help me, even though in so doing, she was sacrificing an evening in the Badgers' Holt.

Delilah and I had arranged to meet for a quick dinner at Frascati before applying ourselves to the task in hand. We settled for pizzas, as I must confess, with the exception of the breakfast calzone, Ed's pizzas are particularly good. He makes the crusts sublimely thin without a hole in sight and the toppings were in exactly the right proportions and combinations.

Delilah was wearing a pink mohair jumper and some designer jeans; most incongruous for the task we were about to complete. There was also a distinct lack of Bertie. She explained that she had promised to meet Sergeant Claringdon in the pub for last orders – *'interesting'* I had said, smiling. Delilah was at pains to tell me she was going to *'gather information'* on the progress of the investigation and had no interest in the sergeant whatsoever. I did feel a little sorry for the man but at the same time Delilah's protestations were a little too forceful to be entirely true. Perhaps the dapper sergeant had finally succeeded in interesting Miss Delibes?

Appetites now sated, we went to leave, but our progress was impeded by Ed. Concerned that we were not having our usual dessert of tiramisu, he wanted to know if the pizzas had not been up to scratch. We explained our mission and he even volunteered to help us, but we declined.

I found this offer most strange, as Fridays are easily one of his busiest evenings. I think his offer was based on Delilah's presence, as opposed to any true altruism. He insisted on takeaway cappuccinos, on the house, to aid us with the evenings work and we headed off across the road to the allotments and Mary's caravan.

Mary's allotment looked none the worse for a week without maintenance. It seemed a shame that soon it would be dug over and the plants that Mary had careful chosen for their various properties would be no more.

Picking our way down the path, carefully past the nettle patch, I noticed the Aloe veras were starting to look brown, a consequence of being protected from the rain outside and therefore starved of water. I made a note to take one home with me as Mary had told me they were very good for burns and scalds. It would be a waste for all these plants to simply be thrown on a compost heap, after Mary had spent so much time caring for them.

Unfortunately, the wetter weather had done nothing to slow the process of decay and a wall of smell met us as we opened the caravan door. The windows had been closed tight for almost a week and now the fruit and herbs used in Mary's recipes were beginning to form their own colonies.

Mary's caravan consisted of two rooms. The main living space included a fold down bed and on the far side a kitchen area. The second room was hardly a room. It contained a shower and a chemical toilet, which I'm pleased to say, had been kept very clean. A recluse but not entirely adverse to modern amenities, Mary had had electrics installed and the generator whirred into action as the main light was turned on.

We started clearing the gate-legged table first, wanting to rid ourselves of any unnecessary olfactory company. It made sense, therefore, to start with item of furniture emanating the most smell. Mary had used this area for making her herbal teas. It was the furthest away from the door and stood at the far end of the caravan, underneath a small window. Only one side of the table extended towards us.

Delilah was used to the smell of decay and started to place the mouldy apples, dried flowers, crisp stalks and leaves of Mary's herb stock into one of the black plastic bags we had brought with us. She held them at arms length so as not to soil her clothing and her expression was one of curiosity as she examined the occasional item to establish its origin.

We were halfway through clearing the top of the table when I recognised something of interest, just as Delilah plucked it from the pile. Urging her to stop, with a shout that was perhaps a little too loud given the proximity of my assistant, I reached forward and took the dried bit of plant from her thumb and forefinger.

'Digitalis' I announced. I held the plant up to the evening light of the window to examine it further.

Delilah peered at it with me, 'It certainly looks like it, but I'm hardly surprised Blake. You told me Mary collected all sorts for her potions and pills.' Delilah's knowledge of horticulture was growing.

The dried brown flowers of the foxglove, now well out of season, hung limply from their stem, a shadow of their former beauty.

'To my knowledge, if any part of the Digitalis plant is ingested it could be deadly.' I said.

There was silence as we stared at the offending flora. As I held the plant aloft in front of us, I wondered as to its significance. Why would Mary be so careless with such a poisonous plant? She didn't even grow foxgloves. In fact, I remember she was very careful to pull them up and dispose of them whenever they did grow on her plot. They are very easily confused with *Symphytum officinale* or common comfrey.

Outside the drill of a nightjar brought me back to the room.

'So what is it doing here in amongst the leaves she uses for her blackberry tea?' I said, out loud this time.

'Beats me.' Delilah said. 'Hang on, isn't Digitalis something to do with the heart? Mary died of a heart condition, didn't she?'

Delilah was correct. *Digitalis purpurea*, or the Foxglove as it is commonly known, has a long history of use in medicine. Digoxin originates from the Foxglove and is a well-known drug used for treating arrhythmias. But it is prescribed in minute, controlled doses.

'They said it was natural causes, so I suppose it could have been her heart.' I muttered, almost to myself. 'But it doesn't feel right. She used her herbs for a variety of things, and I know that she made and took her own tablets, but I don't think she would have been silly enough to self-administer Digoxin. She still respected doctors despite her homeopathic tendencies.'

'You and your feelings!' Delilah shook her head. 'Sometimes people are just as they seem Blake. Perhaps Mary was a deluded crackpot. Maybe she did use the Digitalis and maybe that's what got her in the end.'

I pondered the strange addition to the table whilst Delilah ploughed on with the clearing. I felt sure Mary would not be that stupid. It also puzzled me that there appeared to be only one piece of this plant, just sitting in amongst the blackberry leaves. I was pretty sure her Blackberry tea did not include this plant. Involuntarily, I raised my hand to my throat, hoping I had not been drinking Digitalis all this time.

Not wanting to part with the plant just yet, I placed it in one of the empty jars lined up along the draining board of the tiny kitchenette. Returning to the table, I again became immersed in our task.

As we continued I wondered what Mary would think of it all. I'd like to think she would not have minded the idea of giving any valuables to a worthy cause. Delilah and I had settled on a charity that reunited missing people with their families; it seemed apt. As we gathered items of value from amongst the general chaos of the caravan, we placed them in an empty cardboard box we'd found under the gate-leg table. The rest we left for clearance.

By ten o' clock, the box contained a set of first edition books referencing the healing properties of herbs, some pearls and costume jewellery I'd found in a case by Mary's bed, a brass desk lamp, a framed cross stitch sampler, a camel hair coat, still in very good condition, some everyday Delftware, probably not that valuable and a 1920's sunburst mirror.

By the time I got to the small writing table, to the left of the door in the main living area, I was tiring a little of our work. Delilah too was beginning to get restless. Last orders at the Badgers' Holt were calling. Opening the top drawer of the table, I began to check through its contents. Almost immediately, I found a small notebook filled with various recipes, one of which was Blackberry Leaf Tea, thankfully without Foxglove! I thought Mary wouldn't mind if I was to keep that for myself to peruse at my leisure and I slipped it into my coat pocket before continuing.

In the next drawer, a fob watch lay on top of some papers and, in removing it to place in the box for charity, my eye fell on a paper that sat on top of the pile - a thin yellow carbon copy of a form.

I was alerted to its importance by the words HM PRISON SERVICE stamped in the top left hand corner. What interested me further still was the prisoner's name: DEVINE. Delilah became aware of my curiosity in what was clearly a visiting order and came over to join me by the bureau. The order dated back to last year when, I assumed, Devine was still languishing in a secure prison.

'Well, well, well' she said looking over my shoulder. 'So Mary went to see Reuben Devine in prison. You didn't tell me she was mixed up with that lot. I'm surprised at you Blake, mixing with criminals.' She smirked and nudged me with her elbow.

Bristling at her implication, and the fact that I had not known of Mary's relationship with the Devines, I felt impelled to justify myself and I replied,

'I had no idea. Mary made no reference to Reuben Devine at all and she rarely spoke to Samphire, or at least that's what she had me believe.'

Delilah laughed and started to tie up the black plastic bags She stopped as she caught sight of herself in a mirror and muttered something about looking like a haystack; I refrained from making any comment on the Mohair jumper.

As we tidied up the last few bits and pieces I slipped the visiting order into my pocket with the recipe book and began to think about the various conversations I'd had with Mary. She had only ever mentioned the Devines when she wanted to tell me how atrocious it was that one of the allotments belonged to a criminal. And she only ever mentioned Samphire by name when it was in the same sentence as a complaint about her positively wild allotment - another irony that had not passed me by.

The replaying of conversations in my head was interrupted by the slam of a car door from the previously silent night outside. The allotments were normally deserted at this time, since there was no sensible way to garden at night. Two headlights glared at us from the car park. As they faded there was another thump of a car door, I assume, a passenger.

'I wonder who that is?' Delilah rushed to turn the lights off plunging us into darkness. She walked back across the room and peered through the grubby caravan window.

My eyes gradually adjusted to the dark.

'Given recent events,' I replied, 'It's probably best not to ask. Maybe we should finish this another time, there's not much left to do and it's very dark now.' I did not fancy another moonlight escapade, ending in further injury, in order to save Delilah from certain doom. 'Sergeant Claringdon will be waiting for you won't he? Perhaps I should walk you across to the Badgers' Holt.'

'What and miss out on all the fun? Oh no, don't give me all that fluff! If I know you Blake, you're going to go and see who that is. Come on, lets go!' She was out the caravan door before I could say *serial killer*.

Picking my way across the dark allotments, I tried to catch up with her as fast as my foot would allow. In my attempt to catch Delilah, I'd rashly left my cane propped up against the gate-leg table. Eventually, I reached the car park with Delilah only a second or two ahead. The vehicle was in darkness and I'm pleased to say empty, but it was easy to see that glint of the gold paintwork belonging to Derek Nyeman's van. The obvious questions sprang to mind: what was he doing here at this time of night? And given the slam of two car doors, who was he here with?

The Lily

The lily was sacred to the Greeks, as it was believed to have grown from the milk of Hera, who was the queen of the gods. In association with death, the lily represents the restored innocence of the soul.

We stood for a moment beside the van, peering into the darkness. The clouds had drifted over the moon and the allotments were now pitch black. The only light came from the street lamps lining the High Street in the distance behind us.

The pillow of cloud dulled the sound of voices, but it was still unmistakeable. The distinctive nasal tones of Derek Nyeman were easily picked out, accompanied by a much deeper, second voice. The conversation, I could not decipher. The voices were a short distance away and they echoed slightly. I deduced they were heading down the alley to Poets Avenue. The raised voice of Nyeman's companion suggested it was not necessarily a friendly conversation.

What kind of clandestine affair was the man up to this time? Nyeman's professional troublemaking knew no bounds but I preferred to think it was something to do with the right-of-way, rather than any murderous intent. Perhaps the other voice was a councillor or a fellow saboteur.

Reluctant to go looking for trouble, I suggested we return to the caravan, lock up and return home. Or in Delilah's case, the Badgers' Holt for her date, for which she was now fifteen minutes late. It is conceivable that with the darkness of the night and the memory of murder still fresh in our minds, we were perhaps getting carried away. For all we knew Nyeman might well park his van at the allotments every night, so that protest boards were to hand for his morning ramble. However, in the back of my mind I knew I did not see it parked here every morning.

I offered to finish tidying the caravan myself so that Delilah could go and meet Sergeant Claringdon. She reluctantly agreed on the proviso that I report back on any further allotment shenanigans tomorrow morning, when we were to attend the funeral of the late Mrs Devine. I did not mind finishing up in the caravan; part of me was curious to see if Delilah would manage to winkle any more information out of the sergeant. Besides, spending your evening with an old man clearing a musty caravan cannot possibly be high on young lady's list of pressing engagements.

Once Mary's little abode was left in some semblance of order, I retrieved an Aloe Vera plant from the lean-to, locked up and headed home to an uneasy night's sleep. Perhaps my restless night was due to worry with regard to Delilah's amateur sleuthing. Maybe it was Nyeman's meeting that preoccupied me, or did I have a guilty conscience? Yet again, I would be spending time absent from my shop and this time in favour of attending the funeral of a woman I did not know. Excuses just seemed come easier these days. I was even starting to receive the odd telephone call for customers enquiring as to when the shop would be open.

Snapping my aching bones back into place, I arose, pulled on my dressing gown and ate my usual breakfast of Special K. It had been my wife's favourite, and sentiment meant I had never changed. As I said before, my brain had been active for most of the night, as my dreams had played through the various possibilities. The task of masticating the flakes helped me to think. By concentrating on the rise and fall of my jaw as I ate, I was able to meditate and consider the meaning of my night's dreaming.

The meeting Delilah and I had overheard the night before had been replayed several times - only in the dreams, I could see the faces. In one, it had been the Mayor that Nyeman was talking to and in another Major Turnball. The strangest of all was the presence of Peter Kürbis. Not a gruesome spectre as one might expect but as he would have appeared minus the pumpkin; happily talking to the activist rambler. The two things they all had in common were the presence of Nyeman and the absence of sound. Unable to determine what they were talking about, the only thing that was clear to me was that the events of the past few weeks had become jumbled in the filing system of my hippocampus.

On finishing my breakfast, I continued to get ready for the day ahead, whilst pondering the significance of my dream's inhabitants. The presence of the Mayor was easily explained by his involvement in the dispute over the right-of-way. He was a stalwart supporter of our allotments and he has, in the past, had heated words with Derek Nyeman. Then there was, the presence of Major Turnball with his well turned out appearance, manicured moustache and trademark Homburg. Again, he was a supporter of the allotments, but I had never seen him associate with Derek Nyeman; ever.

The appearance of Peter Kürbis in my rêve can only have been my association between Nyeman and the murders. But did I really think he was capable of it? We now have evidence that Nyeman has been parking by the allotment at night. We already know he has violent tendencies, or perhaps that was only when faced with decisions regarding millet. A man can have an off day one supposes. However, in my experience, Nyeman was off most days.

Moreover, if I was trying to make sense of these dreams, if I really did believe my brain was trying to relay a message from my subconscious to the here and now, what would any of them be doing at the allotment at that time of night? There was no doubt about it though. Last night we had seen Nyeman's van and moreover heard his voice on the allotments late at night. Two deaths in quick succession seemed to be enough to put most people off hanging around the plots in the dark. Unless, of course, you had a desire to be murdered, accused of it, or even commit a second murder…or in my opinion third. My heart raced at the thought.

I turned my mind to less morbid thoughts. I wondered how Delilah's meeting with Sergeant Claringdon had gone. Had she got the update she wanted? Were the police any further forward with the investigation? Had the sergeant seen through her ruse? Had Delilah told Claringdon about the visiting order or the Digitalis? Both these things, in my opinion were relevant to the case and an exchange of information might glean a more elaborate response from Claringdon.

I had every intention of handing this information over but I had been tired last night and waiting a few hours would make little difference. I felt sure Claringdon would be at the funeral today, given the possibility of Reuben Devine's appearance. I would take my opportunity then.

It was a very small funeral. Twelve people attended including Delilah and myself. Most of the family I did not recognise as residents of Tuesbury, but I understood from my brief conversations with Samphire that only Reuben Devine had chosen to live here. The rest of his family lived in Berkshire and Essex. The police were, as I expected, present but at a respectful distance.

Delilah and I stood beside the grave in readiness for the priest's homily. Samphire was dressed in a very dignified black, capped sleeved shift dress. An oversized black straw hat, adorned with a net bow and cascading net veil shading her face. Delilah had chosen a black 1950's style dress with, I'm afraid to say, another hatinator. Thankfully, not as flamboyant as some creations I've seen her wearing, but her love of these particular fashion accessories has me despairing.

The hoped-for appearance of Reuben Devine, did not transpire. I'm not sure this is at all surprising given the man is on the run. To turn up at a funeral, when there is every likelihood the police will expect you to be there, is probably a little imprudent. I was disappointed that Reuben Devine valued his freedom over the funeral of his mother. On the other hand the ceremony did uncover a far more interesting family member.

As I had made my way along the High Street towards the church, I had not thought much about our home from home, Frascati, being closed. However I was curious about Ed's presence at the funeral. Not only was he there, but he was also a pallbearer.

Delilah too seemed surprised. I would have expected Ed to mention his association with the deceased, at least in passing, to her. His apparent affection for her might have encouraged him to play the sympathy card, which in the case of Delilah might just have worked.

He surprised me further, during the service, by choosing to stand on the opposite side of the grave to Samphire. He was stood instead with a man about the same age as myself but they did not talk. Ed's feet were turned slightly towards the man suggesting he was concerned for his well-being although there was no physical offer of consolation, as you may expect at a funeral.

As the priest spoke of a better place, the family bowed their heads and dabbed their eyes with white tissues, bright against the sombre shades of black, brown and grey. Delilah placed an arm around Samphire and dropped lilies into the grave at the appropriate moment. Samphire nodded in thanks. Lilies have always had an unfortunate association with death but they can mean so much more than an end - a regained innocence and purity that perhaps is only truly ours once we have left this life.

At the end of the service, Delilah approached Ed to offer her condolences. I thought it best to hang back, as no-one wants to be crowded at the funeral of a loved one, well-wishers or not. I was close enough to hear the conversation and I soon learned that Ed was Reuben Devine's cousin. Matilda Devine, once Matilda Malani, had been his aunt.

Ed explained that he was reluctant to make his association with the Devines public knowledge, as he was aware of their reputation in the village, but he'd wanted to support his father and say goodbye to his aunt in the proper fashion. I'd never thought about Ed's surname before. I'd only ever seen it above the door of his café identifying him as the licensee. Even if I had, I still would not have made the connection. I had no knowledge of the late Mrs Devine's maiden name, nor had I thought it to be of any significance.

Ed invited us back to the café where the wake was to be held and it would have been churlish to refuse. As we made our way through the grey stones and bright flowers of the graveyard, he told us about the times he'd spent with his aunt and games he and his cousin had played in the garden of his aunt's house. Hearing him speak of Reuben with such affection made me wonder why they were not still good friends.

I asked if he still spoke to Reuben and he became very serious explaining that he had not spoken to him since his cousin had chosen a life of crime. As a businessman in the village, he could not afford to have his name associated with the Devines. He asked Delilah and I for our discretion on the matter, to which we agreed.

As we reached the edge of the church grounds and the lych-gate leading to the High Street, Detective Sergeant Claringdon approached with Detective Constable Alston.

'Miss Delibes.' He nodded in Delilah's direction and she smiled. Alston shuffled beside him, uncomfortable as always. 'Mr Malani, I wondered if we might have a word?' He continued.

'What *now*? Can't it wait?' Ed replied, justifiably indignant.

'I'm afraid not Mr Malani,' the sergeant said.

'Rob,' Delilah said, visibly surprising both Ed and the detectives with the use of the sergeant's first name; deliberately no doubt. Linking her arm through Ed's she continued, 'perhaps this could wait until after the wake?'

Once again, I found myself feeling sorry for the hapless policeman. No one wishes to have his or her authority challenged in such a manner, especially not by someone wearing a hatinator.

Claringdon nodded and cleared his throat.

'Perhaps it would be better if we could speak to you later this afternoon?' He said, trying his best to ignore the heat emanating from his cheeks. 'We do have some questions concerning your relationship with the Devines.'

'I don't see how it's relevant, Sergeant.' Ed replied, 'But if you insist.' Ed unlinked his arm from Delilah's and tugged at his ear lobe.

'I do, and it really would be easier all round if you co-operated' Claringdon said

'You're starting to make me sound like a criminal.' Ed laughed nervously and scratched his nose, 'I can assure you I know very little about my cousin's business dealings,' he said shoving his hands firmly into his pockets and moving closer to Delilah again.

She was standing arms folded, observing the discomfort of Sergeant Claringdon. I, on the other hand, was far more interested in the discomfort of Ed. It was far more than the general embarrassment that most people felt on being approached by the police. From where I was standing I could see small beads of sweat accumulating on his forehead and he was blinking far too often. No, he was nervous about something.

'Nonetheless,' Sergeant Claringdon said, 'you may have some useful information that would help us in finding him.'

'Of course. Come to the café around three and I'll be happy to answer any questions.' Ed finished a little too quickly, immediately stepping through the lych-gate and onto the High Street before the sergeant could reply. Delilah followed and I took my opportunity.

'Might I have a word sergeant' I asked smiling, my voice cracking slightly as I broke my silence. With the service and the presence of a talkative Delilah, I had not spoken for some time; simply observed.

'Of course Mr Hetherington.' He replied appearing far more amiable than he had on previous encounters.

I indicated to Delilah and Ed that they should continue on and I'd catch up. I started to tell the two detectives about Mary's caravan, the visiting order, the

Digitalis and my belief that her death may not have been due to natural causes.

His reply of '*Really*' to this last proposition was little too sarcastic for my liking but I chose to overlook it, as he seemed to show great interest in the visiting order. I promised to bring it to the police station later that afternoon so that he may follow it up. In hindsight, perhaps it was asking a little too much to expect him to pay too much heed to the ramblings of an old man talking about herbs and poisoning. After all, had I not thought a similar thing of Mary and her homeopathic remedies? A little bite from karma.

As I walked down the High Street towards Frascati, I found I was once more left with many questions; even a few hypotheses, but no real facts.

I still did not know what Nyeman had to do with all of this, if anything. It could well be that he is simply an interfering busybody intent on troublemaking. His only motive for murder was the right-of-way. I really could not see what he would gain from murdering Kürbis or Mary, if she had, as I suspected, been murdered.

I felt sure that she had been poisoned, and very possibly with Digitalis in her blackberry tea. If this was the case then why? Was I too a target? I often drank the tea with her. Did the killer know that? I quashed that idea quickly and told myself I was being silly; unnecessarily scaring myself.

Then there was the visiting order. What was Mary's connection with the Devines? Why on earth was she visiting Reuben Devine in prison? Furthermore, he would have had to send her the visiting order, thereby requesting her presence.

Finally, what was Ed hiding? His behaviour had been very peculiar when speaking to Claringdon, very different from his normal confident cheerful attitude.

Granted he had just buried his aunt but his protests were more than indignation, they were bluster. Why had he tried so hard to hide his association with his cousin?

I found the excuse of reputation hard to swallow, considering many didn't even know who Reuben was. He'd been in prison for a long time. Was Ed in fact still friends with his cousin despite what he had told us? Had he told Reuben about his wife's affair? Did Claringdon know something about Ed and his cousin?

And there it was, the light bulb moment - was Ed, Reuben's man on the outside?

The Apple:

Malus x domestica, or the humble apple as it is more commonly known, has played its part throughout history: representing temptation in the Garden of Eden, love in the time of King Solomon, eternal youth to the Norsemen and the culture of peace in China.

The theft of a golden apple from the Greek goddess Hera's garden is said to eventually have been responsible for the start of Trojan War. To this day people still refer to it as *'the apple of discord'*.

The next day, Frascati was heaving. Sunday mornings mean late breakfasts: fry-ups to soak up the previous night's debauchery, bachelors with nothing in the fridge and mothers catching up over coffee whilst their children play *'Sunday Soccer'*. Despite the small size of the café, Ed packed them in, in a clever Tetris of tables and chairs.

I had intended to open the shop that Sunday to make up for the missed trade on previous days. But once more I had given in to procrastination and not opened. I was weary from the last few days' activities. Instead I had absolved my conscience slightly by taking the top hats home with me to complete the family crests.

I was due to meet Delilah at ten thirty; it was now eleven and she was yet to turn up. This was not entirely unexpected and I had the Sunday paper to keep me busy. A late morning coffee meant a late review of the obituaries. This morning, I had found little in the announcements to pique my morbid curiosity.

However, a small article beside the obituaries *had* taken my attention.

It was only a few lines but nevertheless they were significant. A well known local botanist had died from ingesting the leaves of the Digitalis plant - only two but it had been enough to slow his heart to the extent necessary to allow him to shuffle off in his sleep several hours later. The authorities were unable to reach a verdict as to his death; was he murdered or was it suicide? A most unusual and clearly very sad case. It was, exactly the sort of evidence I needed to persuade Claringdon that Mary was murdered! She would never have administered the plant to herself, I was sure of it.

Delilah entered the café forty minutes late, just as I was finishing my coffee so I folded my paper up carefully with the botanist's story uppermost. After hanging her fleece on the back of the chair opposite me, Delilah approached the counter to order two more coffees and for herself, poached egg on toast.

'On a diet' she replied to my ever so slightly raised eyebrow, at the lack of breakfast calzone.

I had no reply to that; diet is a tricky subject of conversation with a lady. Do you reply – *'But you don't need to go on a diet'* and risk an in depth account of that lady's reasons for dieting, have them think you are patronising them, or worse still the assumption that you are not just being kind but flirting. Or do you reply *'Well it's about time too'*? I think we know how that would end and no gentleman with an ounce of breeding, or a strong desire to live, would say that to the female of the species. Changing the subject, I pointed to the article I had just found.

'Mary was murdered.' I said, pushing the paper in Delilah's direction. The café was busy with chatter and I had to raise my voice slightly to be heard by her. For once though, there was no danger of anyone eavesdropping on our conversation so I felt it safe to talk on the subject.

Delilah digested the article until her poached eggs arrived. She handed the paper back to me replying.

'So your instinct is right again Blake, but if Mary was murdered, who on earth did it?' and she began to tuck into her breakfast.

Delilah eating was about the only time I had an extended period in which to speak. I am not often prone to monologues, I prefer instead the ideas created through conversation but I needed to air my findings so far. I began to explain my lines of thinking and the many questions I had amassed.

Why was Mary killed? Did she know something? Had I been a target too, given that I also drank the tea? What was Mary's connection with the Devines? Was Kürbis killed because he was having an affair? And what was Mary's connection with Kürbis? Had the same knowledge resulted in their demise?

I chose to omit my suspicions in regard to Ed at this point. In truth I was not sure how attached Delilah was to the amiable proprietor but I suspected perhaps not as much as he was to her. Delilah's love life, thankfully, remained a mystery to me. However, until I had some hard evidence that Ed was involved in this mystery, I was reluctant to cast aspersions just yet.

Delilah listened patiently, occasionally contributing with an, 'are you sure?' or a 'hmmm'. I finished my conjecture as Delilah finished her breakfast. Placing the knife and fork carefully together on the plate, she dabbed her mouth with a napkin. Now it was her turn. She took a deep breath and began.

'I can't help feeling we're missing something really obvious here Blake. I don't believe Reuben Devine would get his hands dirty murdering people and even if he did, you have to ask why? If you ask me, I think it's all to do with this missing artefact Professor Malus told me about. If Peter knew about it, perhaps Mary did too?'

On mentioning the artefact, I leaned forward frowning; I must have mentally misfiled the information about the black market angle. It had not been mentioned again and perhaps I'd been distracted by Mary's death, the show, the funeral and the caravan. But yes, perhaps they both had known about the hypothetical artefact.

'That's it Delilah! Brilliant, that has to be it'. I sat back in my chair and began to connect the dots. What followed was a waterfall of words, most unusual for me, but I could finally see the light at the end of the tunnel.

'Of course! The allotment links Peter and Mary. The Devines own an allotment but Samphire, at least, has no knowledge of gardening of any kind. That, in itself, is suspicious. The Devines must have another use for their allotment. Peter was having an affair with Samphire, perhaps she told him something? Mary visited Reuben in prison so did she know something too? The knowledge must have related to this hypothetical artefact; that's the thing that could link all three. Reuben must have had someone on the outside, someone he trusted, as you say he probably wouldn't want to get his hands dirty himself, which means...'

It was here I once again reached the conclusion I had last night only, this time the black holes were slowly filling with dark matter. Delilah hadn't heard anything past 'Of course'... apparently I'd started muttering and the general hubbub in the café had drowned out my voice. The noise had reached a crescendo as the football mothers had all said goodbye to one another, left together and in so doing emptied half the café.

Lost in my thoughts, I had reached my conclusion and, I confess, was rather proud that I had finally found the link, however hypothetical. My ramblings reached their destination and the door to the kitchen swung open as I announced with gusto:

'It must have been *Ed*!'

Delilah's eyes widened as a hand reached in-between us to retrieve the empty yolky plate.

'Did someone mention my name?' Ed smiled down at me.

The silence was palpable and perhaps a little too long. As always, Delilah rescued us with a feminine flutter of her eyelashes.

'The eggs Ed, it must have been the way you cooked them that made them so delicious. I've never had quite such lovely poached eggs.' She beamed at him as he looked down on us with steady dark eyes and a half smile. Turning to me, Delilah continued.

'Are you finished there Blake?' she said indicating my half empty coffee cup. 'Shall we walk over to the allotment and check the radishes.' A weak excuse but one I grabbed. In my opinion retreat was definitely the best option.

I was standing before I made my reply, 'Good idea' I said handing Ed a twenty-pound note. We exited, swiftly leaving Ed, open mouthed, with a healthy tip and, I should imagine, a few questions.

Once outside, Delilah and I hurried towards the allotments.

'Are you sure?' she said as we crossed the main road. '*Ed*? I know he's related to criminals but a murderer, *really*?' She was speaking in almost a whisper that my old ears could only just catch over the noise of a car passing behind us.

'It's the only explanation' I said. 'Reuben needs a man on the outside, someone he can trust. Who better than his cousin?'

Delilah nodded 'But what's Ed's motive? I can't see him killing people based on the whim of his cousin. He just doesn't seem the type.'

It was about here in the conversation that I realised Delilah had not heard some of my concluding in the café. As I had suspected some time ago, Delilah's criminal radar was not working. It was one of the frustrating dichotomies of personality that she had: the first being that she spoke so much and yet frequently did not listen; the second that she took such an interest in murder yet never suspected anyone capable of it.

By this time, we'd reached the gate of the allotments and I turned to face my comrade who, despite my limp, was a foot behind me, still reeling from the latest revelations.

'Ed knew about Peter and Samphire, yes?' I started.

'Yes', replied Delilah.

'Reuben and Samphire own an allotment here.' I said indicating the plots.

'OK', replied Delilah.

'Professor Malus implied that Reuben had something valuable left over from his burglaries.'

'Correct.'

'Maybe the missing item is hidden on the allotment? Perhaps Peter knew about it and perhaps Mary did too. She must have visited Reuben for *some* reason, yes?'

'Yes.'

'Perhaps Ed knew Samphire had shared this knowledge with Peter and Ed told his cousin. Reuben might have asked Ed to 'deal' with it.'

'Ahhhh. But murder?'

'Or maybe Ed wanted the artefact for himself? Perhaps he's not working for his cousin at all? Perhaps, as are most criminals, he is simply self-serving and, ultimately, greedy.'

There was a cough from the other side of the gate that interrupted our clandestine conversation. Looking up we were presented with the tall, suited and muddy-shoed vision of Detective Sergeant Claringdon.

'Perhaps he is.' Replied the sergeant.

I made a mental note: we really had to start being more careful about where we discussed these things.

It was then we took in the scene. How we hadn't noticed it on our approach I do not know. My only excuse was we were deep in conversation and somewhat preoccupied with the thought that we'd just had breakfast served to us by a murderer.

Given the amount of police officers on the allotments it was surprisingly quiet. Ant like, they carefully ferried pieces of evidence backwards and forwards from the Devine's shed, in almost complete silence. The occasional laugh or cough was all that could be heard from the gate. The sergeant placed his hands in his pockets and went to speak once more. He was interrupted before he could start.

'Sarg', a call came a WPC stood in the doorway of the Devine's shed. In her hand was something large and wrapped in what looked like an old curtain. She was waving the sergeant over.

'You two had better come with me', Claringdon said looking at us as though we were a couple of naughty school children who'd just been caught vandalising the bike sheds. Neither of us felt inclined to argue. In the light of our recent discovery, I think we were, on this occasion, grateful for police escort.

Claringdon left us a few steps back from the Devine's allotment with strict instructions not to move. We obeyed and watched as a brief discussion occurred between the sergeant and his officer. There was some gesticulating and craning of necks at whatever was in the old curtain fabric. Was this our artefact, so tantalising close? Delilah and I were transfixed. The sergeant put some gloves on, took the curtain and its contents from the officer, and walked across to us.

He quickly revealed his intention.

'Miss Delibes, I'm given to understand that you know about artefacts?' He said this in such a matter-of-fact way that Delilah was a little taken aback. Used to having the upper hand with men, especially Sergeant Claringdon, the formality and directness of the request visibly unnerved her.

'Yes sergeant,' she replied gaining her composure and maintaining the official air of the conversation.

'What can you tell me about this?' he said holding forward the object still nestled in its curtain.

There was no other word for it - it was beautiful: a large and carefully crafted box, about twelve by fourteen inches in size. Despite the obvious patina from years of wear that dulled it, the ornate carving on its cover, in what I assumed to be gold or, at the very least, gold leaf still shone through. It reminded me of the illuminated scripts I have seen in cathedrals and churches.

Strange mythical animals danced around the outside, whilst in the middle was the figure of what I now know to be a Saint. This was clearly an item of great value and I wondered if this was the artefact once belonging to Professor Malus? The item appeared solid, although I was not privileged enough to handle it or get very close; unlike Delilah who was now peering into the curtain.

'I'm not so sure' Delilah said. 'I've never seen anything quite like this before. I have seen similar pieces of course, but nothing of this quality and I'm not an expert in this kind of thing.' She was trying hard to contain her excitement and remain in control of her emotions in front of the sergeant.

She paused, frowning at the artefact, and chewed her fingernail. Her breathing was steady as she concentrated, and the gold from the cover reflected in her brown eyes. Not once did she look up at the sergeant, instead giving her complete attention to the object resting in his hands.

'But what is it?' Sergeant Claringdon's frustration showed through. He was a man used to getting answers quickly and Delilah appeared to be obtuse in this matter.

Now she chose to look up. Sensing the sergeant's frustration, she had the upper hand once more. Smiling, she began slowly to tell us what I suspect she had known from the moment she saw it.

'Well, if I'm right sergeant, I think it's the case for some kind of religious book. They were often made out of gold or silver, sometimes more than one copy was made but this one looks very grand. Much grander than anything I've seen before. Perhaps it's the great gospel of Colmcille or St Columba as he's better known.' She paused for a response but got none. The sergeant was well used to playing this game.

Unable to resist showing off, Delilah continued, this time with her usual rapidity and more obvious enthusiasm, 'It was the cover of the Book Of Kells, which you'll find in Dublin if you're interested. The Book of Colmcille was stolen in A.D 1006 and although it was returned, the gold cover was never seen again. Perhaps this is it? I happen to know someone who might be able to tell us.' Finishing her speech she folded her arms and looked for the sergeant's reaction.

'As I thought', he replied, smiling at her.

So there it was: a very likely motive for two murders. It had been there all along. Nestled in its tatty old curtain, hundreds of years old. Our golden apple!

The Cucumber

Isaiah 1:8 - *'and the daughter of Zion is left as a cottage in a vineyard, as a lodge in a garden of cucumbers, as a besieged city.'*

The lodge mentioned in Isaiah is considered to be the ramshackle hut often found in the Nile Valley or the Levent. The hut is where the watchman would sit to watch over his precious fruit and vegetables. The reference to cucumbers is because Cucurbits grow well near Mediterranean shores and would have been stolen if left unguarded.

An hour later, the allotment was at peace once more. Unlike that fateful day when Kürbis was found face down in my pumpkins, the police had left little evidence of their presence. There was, of course, a reason for this. Claringdon had a plan.

On revealing her knowledge in regard to the shed's treasure, Delilah was now back in control. She had rallied and, in a verbal torrent, apprised the sergeant of our findings and their culmination in the conclusion of a murderous Malani. He took it very well and, in fact, became more amiable once more. We returned with Claringdon to the station where Delilah was to contact Professor Malus. Eventually, Claringdon also shared a few facts.

We were offered drinks from a vending machine and the three of us, Sergeant Claringdon, Delilah and myself, took up seats in a stuffy interview room. The room appeared to have been designed for more informal interviews, but I was still aware of a camera in the corner, watching the foam-cushioned, tired-looking, executive sofas. I risked a murky black tea, not at all like my usual Earl Grey. I placed the plastic cup on a small Formica table before sitting down opposite Delilah and the sergeant. Then the conversation began.

It transpired that since the escape of Reuben Devine, Mrs Devine had been under covert surveillance, as I suspected, in the hope that Mr Devine would contact her. When he had not appeared at the funeral, Claringdon had turned to Ed Malani to answer some questions.

Ed had furnished them with the information that Samphire Devine had been having an affair with Peter Kürbis, a fact the police already knew. What spurred them on to arrest Mrs Devine was the information that she had met Mr Kürbis at Frascati, late on the night of his murder. A fact that Malani had shared, unprompted. Apparently, he had been reluctant to talk earlier as he still felt some loyalty to the Devines. Again, he was eager to point out that he had little to do with the criminal side of his family. So Malani returned to pizza making and the police arrested Samphire.

Once arrested, in fear of her husband's wrath over her affair and hoping for some protection, Samphire had soon told all. She admitted she had been having an affair with Peter Kürbis and expressed remorse - although she had not murdered her lover, she did feel in some way responsible for his demise. She denied the meeting in Frascati. In fact, she insisted that she had not arranged to meet Kürbis that evening, and implied Ed had an ulterior motive for such an accusation.

'The artefact perhaps?' I interjected.

Claringdon nodded and went on to tell us that Samphire did know that her husband had something of great value hidden in the allotment shed. Ed also knew about the artefact.

As a youngster, Ed had hung on Reuben's shirttails following him everywhere and often landing him in all

144

kinds of trouble, which Reuben then had to get them out of. Reuben feared his cousin might bring trouble to their door once more, or worse still make off with the artefact. Believing in the saying - keep your friends close and your enemies closer - Reuben had flattered Ed's ego and made him his informant.

And so it transpired that Ed was still in touch with his cousin despite his protestations at the funeral. It was kept quiet, not because of Ed's business but because that's what Reuben wanted. He did not want his upstart cousin using his name in vain.

For ten years, Samphire had kept the allotment safe for her jailbird husband. Her total lack of interest in gardening had been difficult to explain at times but, like the watchmen of the Levent, she guarded her husband's treasure.

Last year she met Kürbis, and their affair quickly blossomed. In love, she had finally told Peter about the fortune that sat under their very noses. They quickly made a plan to steal it from Reuben and use it to finance their escape abroad; however, Kürbis had been killed before their plan came to fruition.

With Kürbis dead and Reuben on the loose, she had not dared draw attention to herself further by accessing the shed and fleeing with the treasure. Mrs Devine had not seen her husband since he went missing and was glad of this, as she did not want to meet the same fate as her lover.

Samphire suggested that perhaps Reuben was hiding out in some old farm buildings, about five miles northeast of Tuesbury. He and Ed used to play there as children. When searched, there was evidence of Reuben's presence but he was clearly long gone. Therefore, Tuesbury's finest had no alternative but to try and find what was in the shed and hope, in the process, they uncovered some further evidence to tie up the murders.

The use of the word *murders* and not murder almost prompted a response from me at this point. I was still under the impression the police did not think Mary's death was foul play and I was curious as to why Claringdon had referred to multiple murders. The only thing that stopped me was that I had been distracted, with some amusement, as Delilah started to show the detective reserved interest. The odd flick of the hair, the touch of an arm, a softening of the eyebrows and a gentle glow to the cheeks all implied Miss Delibes was actually more taken with the sergeant than she had at first appeared.

As Claringdon reached the end of his story, I was beginning to feel like the proverbial gooseberry. By the end of the conversation they were sitting very close together on the sofa. I shuffled my empty vending machine cup in my hands, unfortunately, making a loud crunching sound, disturbing the atmosphere. Looking up at me, they suddenly became aware of their proximity and instantly moved away from each other. Clearly embarrassed, Claringdon stood up and walked towards the vending machine in the corner of the room.

'Another drink?' he asked. Delilah blushed and nodded as he busied himself with sugar and little milk cartons. I shook my head. One drink from that machine was enough for any lifetime.

'So you agree? Mary was murdered!' I said taking advantage of the lull in discussion.

'Ah, now, your help in that matter was invaluable Mr Hetherington. Had it not been for your amateur sleuthing, Mary's murder might have been completely undetected. I have to say I'm a little disappointed the officers didn't have a better look around the caravan. It's standard practice in a sudden death situation,

146

although perhaps they do not have your horticultural prowess.' Claringdon said.

He was flattering me now, but I have to say I gave a wry smile at this comment. I had been sure the sergeant had discounted my contribution, that day by the gate of the graveyard. Clearly, I was wrong about this young man.

'Mary's death, as you know, at first appeared natural,' he continued, 'until of course Mr Hetherington suggested the use of Digitalis and further still provided us with the evidence. So, naturally, I re-examined the tox report.' His voice was uncertain. 'We can see she did have elevated levels of Digoxin in her blood but I'm not sure how it was done.'

'I might be able to help you there.' I reached into my inside jacket pocket for the folded newspaper article. Thankfully, I had had the presence of mind to take it with me despite our abrupt exit from the café.

Claringdon took the paper from my outstretched hand and returned to the sofa to sit next to Delilah, this time a respectable distance away. He examined the article, stopping only to blow on his hot coffee and take a tentative sip.

'I think the Digitalis was put in Mary's tea.' I said

'Well that could very well be the answer.' He looked up, 'Of course it is circumstantial.'

'What about the cup?' I replied

'Which cup is that?' The sergeant looked puzzled.

'Mary's cup! It was smashed but I pointed it out to one of the officers on the day. I think he put it in one of your evidence bags, although I'm not sure he appreciated my input.'

'I'll get someone onto it now.' He jumped up from the sofa and dashed off down the hall. Delilah and I sat in stunned silence, unsure what to say about the day's events so far. We didn't have to wait long before he was back, this time with doughnuts.

I declined; Delilah did not and spent the next few minutes trying to find a ladylike way to eat it in front of Claringdon.

'So the motive must have been that she knew something, perhaps the same thing as Kürbis?' I ventured whilst the sergeant was licking the sugar from his fingers.

'It's funny you should say that', Claringdon replied, 'Mrs Devine told us that Mary was blackmailing her. Ms Ananassa realised that Samphire knew nothing about gardening and drew her own conclusions on the matter. She never revealed exactly what she knew but it worried Samphire enough for her to pay her blackmailer. Samphire told us that Reuben had been reluctant to part with money when there was no evidence that Mary knew anything. We assume, therefore, that Reuben dispensed with the inconvenient blackmailer. Samphire did not confirm this and we have no evidence, but I doubt a career criminal like Reuben Devine would do his own dirty work…'

'That's what I said,' Delilah interrupted through a mouthful of doughnut. She gave me a satisfied look. The desire to play the *'I told you so card'* clearly outweighed the need to appear refined.

The sergeant continued, 'Mrs Devine has a watertight alibi for Mary's death. Fearing Reuben's wrath, she stayed with her mother for a fortnight after Kürbis's death. So the only person left is Ed Malani, especially given his potentially false statement implicating Samphire.' Claringdon was stirring sugar into his coffee. 'But we still have very little evidence to link Ed Malani or Reuben Devine to either of the murders.' he shrugged.

Delilah returned to the conversation.

'Ed did tell me once that he completed an HND in horticulture before taking over the family business. He'd never wanted to be a chef but, when his father retired, it was expected of him. I felt sorry for him at the time.'

Delilah had regained her composure and was licking her lips and wiping her fingers on a pocket tissue. She blushed as the sergeant looked across at her for just a little too long.

'That would certainly give him the knowledge required,' I replied. It was then that a memory floated to the front of my mind and, in my excitement, I confess I shouted.

'That's it!' Checking myself, I continued a little quieter this time, 'That's what was bothering me.'

The sergeant and Delilah stared at me, in wonderment, from the opposite sofa.

'Ed! The evening before I found Mary, we'd been talking in the cafe about her. Delilah had been having trouble sleeping, most unusual for her.'

Delilah nodded in agreement.

'I'd been telling Delilah about the Vervain tea Mary had made. Mary had said how calming it was with lavender honey. Ed had been delivering a plate of his tiramisu to our table at the time. At the mention of Mary's name he became sentimental. He said, now these were his exact words: *"poor Mary, she always believed in the power of herbs".*' I looked at them both awaiting their realisation.

'And....' Claringdon looked exasperated.

'Believed! He used the word *"believed".*' They still didn't see.

'Past tense! But nobody knew she was dead until I found her the next morning.'

'Brilliant.' Claringdon clapped his hands together but then his shoulders sagged. 'But it's still all circumstantial.' He stared into his coffee appearing to think. 'No, somehow we need to get Malani and Devine together and pray that one of them slips up.'

'How about setting a trap?' Delilah relished this idea and her eyes shone dangerously.

'Entrapment is normally frowned upon in the police force Delilah.' Claringdon replied.

'I know but perhaps if we gave them enough rope….' She said.

'Go on,' Claringdon said.

'Well, how about I tell Ed, that the police have been back on the allotment and that they've found something of interest. Surely that will get him to play his hand?'

Claringdon studied his now empty cup and Delilah waited for her reply.

'OK, that *could* work. I've got a surveillance team watching the shed already. Perhaps pointing Ed in the right direction might just be the impetus he and Devine need. If Ed is Devine's inside man, as we suspect, he'll have to tell him. If we can arrest them together then there's less chance of them concocting a story and more chance that one of them will crack, knowing the other might first.'

'Good!' Delilah looked at her watch. 'It's only half past two,' she said. 'I can go back to the café this afternoon and talk to Ed. Strike while the iron's hot!' Delilah finished by waving her fist in the air.

'Hang on a minute, you're asking Delilah to approach a potential murderer and lure him and his accomplice out into the open?' I was understandably perturbed by this suggestion. Delilah was very naïve when it came to the criminal fraternity and I could not help feeling the sergeant had somehow engineered this. A man that is capable of drawing the conclusions Claringdon had so far, would easily be able to conclude that using an unofficial source to inform Ed, might encourage him to play his hand, whilst avoiding the plea of police entrapment.

'Rob hasn't asked me to do anything. I've volunteered,' Delilah said. 'Don't be such a stick in the mud Blake. I'm only going to talk to Ed - nothing else. You can come too if you'd like, it would be less suspicious if we just turn up for our usual post-allotment tea and scone.' She finished the rest of her coffee, pulling a face at its bitter ending.

So we were back to first names were we? Claringdon was clearly trying to hold the smile from his face at the mention of post-allotment tea and scone. Or maybe it was the success of his manipulation. Neither endeared him to me and the sergeant was once more out of my favour.

The whole idea of inducing a reaction from Ed Malani did not fill me with joy. The last time we'd provoked a murderer, I had come off worse and I had a limited amount of good limbs left. I chose to say nothing. I knew Delilah well enough to know the more I protested the more likely she was to do it anyway.

Claringdon spoke again, 'In the meantime, I'll take the artefact to your Professor Malus to see if he can identify it for us. Let me know as soon as you've spoken to Malani, and Delilah...' The sergeant placed a hand on her knee, 'be careful'.

The Venus Flytrap

Dionaea muscipula, more commonly know as
the Venus flytrap, waits patiently for its prey to
trigger the tiny hairs of its leaves, whereupon its
meal is enclosed in its velvety trap and consumed.

One of the few plants capable of rapid
movement, the Venus flytrap is so called because
its flowers are as hypnotic as the beautiful goddess
Venus.

It was with some discomfort this time that I found
myself, once again, in Frascati with Delilah. Quieter
now the brunch-time rush was over, Ed was once again
thumping dough in the kitchen, in preparation for the
evening's take-away orders. This time the gentle thud
and phut took on a more sinister sound.

Delilah and I had discussed how we might drop the
allotments into any conversation we may have with Ed.
We had not discussed the possibility that he may spend
the majority of his time in the kitchen. To be fair, this
was not usually the case when Delilah was in the café.

Delilah was trying to ease the tension by telling me
all about the dig in Deerton, the finds they had made
and the fact that it was coming to a close next week so
she would soon have to find another project.

We needn't have worried about Ed because he
showed up soon enough.

We had been there for about forty-five minutes
when we heard the phone ring, some mild cursing, the
tap running and Ed finally answering the phone. We
could not hear the conversation in its entirety, but Ed's
raised voice stopped our own conversation in its tracks.
There were four other customers in the café at the time,
some of Nyeman's Rambleteers, but they didn't seem at

all bothered by the kerfuffle in the kitchen. They were engrossed in a map spread out over the table; plotting their next move, no doubt.

The phone conversation ended with a very audible 'OK, OK, I'll bloody sort it!' I'd never heard Ed swear much before. Not that I thought him incapable of it but he'd always been very polite, mild mannered and controlled. In many respects, the quiet man is the one to watch: the man that appears, to all intents and purposes, to be perfectly in control of his emotions. Who knows what repression can lead to? Murder?

He burst out of kitchen, flinging a tea towel around and bellowing 'Everybody out.'

Delilah and I were sat in nervous silence with only the murmurings of the Rambleteers to break the air.

'Everybody out!' Ed shouted again, red-faced and incandescent, as he made his way to the door with the key.

We of course obliged, smiled and said goodbye, leaving the café with feigned nonchalance. Delilah's smile did nothing to break through the ball of fury that was Tuesbury's favourite pizzaiolo and the door slammed behind us, almost jangling the tiny bell off its hook.

I breathed a small sigh of relief that Delilah had been prudent enough not to ask Ed any questions. With no real plan, I suggested we take refuge in my shed up at the allotment, whilst we decided what to do next. We had to find somewhere safe and quickly in order to contact Claringdon, as this development did not fit in with the plan.

If Ed had finally snapped then I, for one, did not want to be close. Who knows what it was he was to 'sort'. He may have been preparing to complete his task as we spoke. Was he planning to murder again? If so, who? Had he discovered the artefact was missing

153

already? Would he go to the allotments as we had intended?

For the second time that day, we found ourselves hurrying across the road. The Rambleteers stood a while on the pavement, looking at their watches, then back at the café. They only moved when the lights inside were turned off, by which time Delilah and I were already back at the gate to the allotments. This time there were no policemen in sight but it was comforting to know they were not far away.

I could just see a black Mercedes in the car park, which I assumed was the Tuesbury constabulary keeping a watchful eye on the allotments. To my dismay, I also saw the gold van of Derek Nyeman. He had started appearing on Sunday afternoons. No doubt to annoy those of us sought peace on our allotments before the week ahead. Now the presence of the Rambleteers in the café made sense. To compound the issue, there was a small group of rucksacked, woolly-socked walkers in the far corner of the allotments and, unfortunately, Derek Nyeman himself.

Like a parliament of rooks with the oldest bird at the centre, Nyeman started to lead his band of ramblers across the plots. Perhaps this is why we did not notice the absence of the original rookery for so long. The cackling of The Rambleteers disguised it. Unlike the rooks, Nyeman's presence was not considered lucky.

As we reached the shed on my allotment, I looked back towards the gate. I noted that the four ramblers from the café, had been joined by three more and they were now executing a pincer movement across the vegetable patches. Now, more than ever, was a reason to seek refuge in my shed.

I am lucky to have a good-sized shed and it is not just a safe haven for my tools. It also includes a sturdy potting bench on which sits a kettle, teabags, a biscuit jar and the small DAB radio. At the far end of the shed I have placed two tatty but comfortable tweed-effect armchairs. They afford a good view of the surrounding plots through a small, cobwebbed window. I see no reason to clean shed windows.

Once Delilah had rung the sergeant to inform him of the recent goings on, we took up our places on the armchairs with a cup of tea and a Maryland cookie to wait for the storm to pass.

The Rambleteers had now gathered at the far end of the allotments and it wasn't long before the men in the Mercedes got out of the car and approached them. They were wearing jeans and short-sleeved shirts but were very clearly police officers, despite their civilian clothes. I was surprised they had revealed themselves given the circumstances, but Nyeman's rabble would certainly deter even the most hardened criminals from entering the allotments.

There was a lot of gesticulating from Nyeman, which included arm waving, finger wagging and folded arms. From what I could see, the officers were getting nowhere and so, unable to reason with the man, they returned to their car; I assume to fry bigger fish.

The police interest had, unfortunately, spurred Nyeman on and he was now herding his Rambleteers onto one of the most central allotments where they all sat down to eat sandwiches and drink from their thermos flasks. The man was a public nuisance and I feared someone might get away with murder simply because Nyeman was an ass!

We had again fallen into talking about Delilah's dig and possible future career options: another Roman villa in West Sussex, an Iron Age settlement in Scotland, Greek ruins in, well, Greece, or a trip to the Antilles to discover the early cultures of the Caribbean. Another half an hour passed when we became aware of a commotion on the Devine's allotment.

Half an hour later the Rambleteers had gone, disappointed by the poor audience and continued lack of interest from the men in the Mercedes. Derek Nyeman's van remained and now a silver Audi had parked on the opposite side of the car park, as far away from the black Mercedes as possible. Although the occupants were not visible from the shed, it was not a car I recognised. I assumed it was another unmarked police car, but I was wrong.

The shouting from the Devines' shed alerted, not only Delilah and I, but also the two officers who were now, once more, out of the car. This time heading across the allotments towards us.

'We're on,' said Delilah rising from the chair. Unable to resist a showdown, she grabbed a fork hanging on the wall and left the shed before I could remonstrate with her.

Once outside, she commenced digging, a pretence that I was reluctant to let her continue with as she was digging up several potato plants that were nowhere near ready. I lurched forward from the shelter of the shed door, my injured foot still unused to sudden movement. I went to remove the fork from her grasp to reduce the damage she was doing. I was just in time to see the door of the Devine's shed fly open and a man I did not recognise exit followed by a shouting, Ed Malani.

'I told you, I haven't got it!' Ed was protesting with an urgency that suggested his life depended on it.

The man he was shouting at was tall with dark hair and a fashionable goatee beard. Overall, he was looking a little unkempt but his shirt was tucked into his jeans and he had an air of importance about him that echoed in Ed's deferential body language.

'Well then, who has?' the man replied.

He turned away from Ed and started towards the car park. I could see the officers were still about a hundred yards away. On seeing them, the man turned back towards Ed and, pointing at the officers, snarled.

'Are they with you, cousin?'

Ed now joined the first man, with a confused look on his face. The pair were silent as they watched the advancing officers who, seeing the exchange, started to pick up pace. The man - whom I now know to be Reuben Devine - started to run in the opposite direction. Ed was still standing near the doorway to the shed, weighing up his options.

The officers were fast approaching but, unfortunately, the mud hindered them and I could see they were not going to get to Reuben in time. Once again it was my civic duty to intervene. One cannot stand injustice and here it was happening right in front of me, so I did the only thing I could. I dropped the fork and ran to intercept him.

All those years of rugby spurred me on. I was not letting this man get away. The goal was in sight and he was not getting a try. My foot throbbed at the exertion and I have to say I stumbled as tried to make my way across the last few feet that separated me from my quarry.

He was almost at the gate, and I was very nearly done for, when who should appear but Derek Nyeman. Where he came from, I still do not know. Maybe he'd been to the High Street to post another letter to the council, or even to the newspaper proclaiming police harassment but either way, the most annoying man on the planet happened to appear at exactly the right time.

Vaulting over the gate, Reuben Devine landed square at the feet of Nyeman and, never one to shy away from a fight, Nyeman promptly punched him square in the face. I can only assume it was instinct. A man travelling at speed and propelling himself over a fence toward you may well prompt the same response in anyone but, as we know, Nyeman had form.

Reuben was out cold and supine in the nettle patch that surrounded the gate to the allotments. Derek was now holding his hand and, with a pained expression, looked up at me. I was by now very out of breath and huffing in a most undignified manner.

'Thank you,' was all I could muster.

'You're welcome,' replied a stunned Nyeman.

I turned to see if Ed was still by the Devine's shed doorway. From what I could see, Delilah had boxed him in with a smile, a torrent of conversation, and the garden fork, thus buying enough time for the police officers to have Ed firmly in custody. Leaving his colleague with Mr Malini and Delilah, the second officer had now reached the gate, just in time for Reuben to regain consciousness with a groan.

Constable Alston looked down at the bemused fugitive.

'Well, well, well, Mr Devine. Fancy seeing you here.'

The Palm Tree

**There are over two thousand different types of
Arecaceae and the palm has played its part
throughout history. The early Christians used the
palm leaf to symbolise the victory of the spirit over
the flesh. Today it is more commonly associated
with the peace and tranquillity of an oasis.**

Derek Nyeman was silent for at least half an hour
after his accidental foray into useful public service.

When he did start talking, it was to point out that a
plaque should be placed on the gate acknowledging him
as the hero of the hour. I saw an opportunity for
negotiation. If a plaque meant an end to his ridiculous
right-of-way campaign, then I was pretty sure the
villagers and allotment owners would agree to this;
anything to silence the menace that threatened our little
plots of heaven.

At the station, we were subjected to yet more plastic
tea and coffee, which I declined, and statements were
taken. It wasn't until the court case, a further eight
weeks later, that the whole truth, and nothing but the
truth, was at last revealed.

Both Delilah and I attended the trial of Ed Malani,
Samphire Devine and Reuben Devine. We were to
stand witness to the events of that October. As the
sergeant had foretold, once arrested, both Ed and
Reuben were eager to tell their own version of the story
in order to implicate the other.

Ed confessed to killing Peter but claimed it was an
accident, as he had not intended to kill him. His lawyer
had been at pains to impress upon the jury that a man
does not choose a pumpkin as a weapon for
premeditated murder? However, new evidence was
presented that proved that Ed had, in fact, planned

Kürbis' death. The toxicology report, completed during the post mortem of Peter Kürbis, had been re-examined and it was discovered that the presence of our old friend Digitalis had been overlooked, again.

The police had come up trumps when, on searching the pizzeria, Ed's stash of dried foxglove was discovered. The prosecution went on to prove that Ed had poisoned Peter and then followed him to the allotments to finish him off. Ed could protest his innocence no longer and so changed his plea to guilty.

The jury found him guilty of premeditated murder, in both cases- that of Peter Kürbis and Mary Ananassa.

Reuben was not so easy to pin down. Malani, although keen to proclaim his innocence, was unwilling to implicate his dangerous cousin. Reuben was very happy to affirm that Ed was the murderer. He claimed had tried to stop him, and how could he be responsible for his cousin's actions?

He was guilty of absconding from prison and attempting to profit from his crimes by hiding the proceeds. Unfortunately, due to his cousin's unwillingness to testify against him, Devine only received a paltry six months in addition to the two months he had left to serve. However I do not think it will be long before Reuben finds himself back in prison. I have a feeling Claringdon is a very determined man.

Samphire Devine did not attend court. She was found guilty of withholding evidence. The judge was, in my opinion, lenient, and in recognition of her assistance in bringing the cousins to justice she was given a suspended sentence and a hefty fine.

The allotments have recovered from the murky murders and zealous police searches. This winter the rookery has even returned. There is now a small plaque on the gate, which reads:

This was a small price to pay for the peace and tranquillity, which has now returned to our plots. Once again the good burghers of Tuesbury can garden in peace.

We are now two weeks away from Christmas and the weather is very different from those days of heady Indian summer almost three months ago. A bitter cold wind is blowing in from the north and a persistent sleet creates a slush of muck and water under foot. I am to go to Devon to visit the grandchildren and spend time with my family. I can safely say that I will be grateful of the rest.

Now the trial is over, Delilah has been spending more time with Sergeant Claringdon. The two of them seem to get on well enough and I'm happy Delilah has found an appropriate suitor at last. I have been told I really should call him Rob when he's off duty. I fear it will take some getting used to; I've always been very respectful of rank, outwardly at least.

Professor Malus did not, for obvious reasons, reclaim the ornate book cover that languished for so many years in the Devines' shed. Delilah's romantic notion that it was the cover of *'The Book Of Colmcille'* was, alas, not so. It is, however, considered to be a fine example of its kind and has now taken its rightful place in an exhibition at the Trinity College Library in Dublin.

Delilah's dig has been completed and she is awaiting news of several placements she had applied for, to start in the spring of next year. In the meantime, she will work on building up the exhibits in the Limehouse Basin museum. The winter weather has encouraged indoor pursuits and she has had several school groups attend the museum in the run-up to Christmas break.

I have, at last, decided to retire. On discussion with my daughter, it has become clear that she, as I suspected, has no desire to take on Hetherington's Hats. Her life is now in Devon with her family and she does not wish to spend the time required to learn the skill of millinery. Nor does she or her family want to move to a '*stinking*' and '*crowded*' London – her words not mine. Personally, I will miss the hustle and bustle of the London streets.

So this will be my last Christmas in Hetherington's Hats and with an – *'Everything Must Go'* sale- it's proving to be a lucrative festive season. I have decided to continue to make bespoke commissions. To give up hats forever would leave a hole in my soul. Delilah and Rob helped me to insulate the shed on my allotment, and I have upgraded the generator so that it is cosy in all weathers. If I am to make hats in a shed, it must be warm with no danger of the damp creeping in.

I now have a small fridge to keep milk in for tea and some new cupboards to keep the articles I am working on safe and dry. My mobile and landline at home serve as a perfectly adequate means of communication with clients. Delilah has even helped me to set up a website and e-mail account, although I am struggling to use these technological wonders.

It was a long time before I discovered that Delilah had called the website *'Hetherington's Mystery Millinery: Bespoke hats and investigative services'*, but that's another story.

COMING HOME FOR CHRISTMAS

A Blake Hetherington Short Story

Party Popped

'I have a message for a Miss Delilah Delibes', the waiter bawled from the bar area; an event most unusual for our favourite pub.

A cheer burst from a crowd of exuberant, dishevelled and drunken office workers, as they started to sing in united discord.

'My, my, my Delilah!'

Christmas had arrived at The Snicket. *Bang!* A balloon popped behind us followed by a second cheer. Such a small pub did not have the capacity for the volume of customers they had squeezed in that evening. The shouting had drowned out the end of my sentence and, adding insult to injury, a stray streamer from a party popper landed on my shoulder; I sighed as I brushed it to the floor. Why could one not go out for a pleasant Christmas meal without being showered in tinsel, glitter and various other festive atrocities?

Delilah raised her hand with her usual effortless confidence, smiling at the waiter and indicating our table. She was celebrating her new job – fieldwork in Haiti - and I was celebrating retirement. The obvious choice had been The Snicket. I was now beginning to regret this decision. Unfortunately, the place wasn't what it used to be. It had once been a small canal side gastro pub near the Limehouse basin. Over the year, it had taken a nosedive towards pleasing the masses. The à la carte menu remained, but now an early bird menu joined it and, sadly, this year a Christmas carvery.

Do not misunderstand me, I do not object to Christmas. I enjoy the celebrations as much as the next man, but I shudder at the thought of carveries. All that meat sitting under hot lights for hours is a veritable playground for bacteria.

It was becoming increasingly difficult to talk over

the noise of the early birds. They seemed intent on celebrating Christmas in a way that seems so popular these days. Drinking as much as possible, as quickly as possible. I'm pleased to say Delilah, in this respect, is a little more demure than many of her age. Or at least she remains so in my company.

Before the waiter's voice had pierced the surrounding din, we had been trying to talk about the year's events. You couldn't make it up. Some of the situations we'd found ourselves in had forged a friendship that was unlikely to falter.

It was with a mixture of sadness and relief that I had locked the door to Hetherington's Hats one last time. With no one to keep the business going and my twilight years fast approaching, I had been forced to ask myself painful questions about the future of my work. I had decided not to sell the premises on the basis that one day it would be my daughter's inheritance. Instead I had found a tenant for the place. A furniture restorer who creates the shabby chic upcycling that is all the rage at the moment.

No more would millinery be a part of that shop. I had been the weak link in the chain of five generations. If Jane had wanted to take over the family business, then things would have been different, but we live in changing times and is millinery really sustainable from a high street store, that incurs London overheads? Besides the newly refurbished shed on my allotment was proving to be more than adequate in order for me to continue making bespoke hats. To leave millinery entirely, as I have said before, would have left a hole in my soul.

Delilah had enjoyed a main of *Turkey with All the Trimmings'* and between the two of us we'd finished a bottle of Sancerre and I suspected a glass of port might be in order next. It was Christmas after all. As I was reminiscing about the shop and lamenting my daughter's reluctance to follow Hetherington tradition, Delilah had been talking about her gentleman follower, Sergeant Claringdon.

'Rob's really not happy about me roughing it in Haiti. I keep telling him we all stay in shared houses these days; we won't be camping. I think the truth is he doesn't like me going away with five men.'

I had nodded. Delilah often talked a lot over dinner and I had taken to offering the odd nod, raise of the eyebrows or twist of the mouth in order to reply and not interrupt my food or, heaven forbid, talk with my mouthful.

' Anyway I'm not going for another three months so I'm sure there's plenty of time for him to get used to the idea.'

Finishing my main of Sea Bream, I replied.

'I'm sure he's only worried about you.'

I felt the need to defend the sergeant. I liked Claringdon. Initially I had not, I confess, but just occasionally my first impressions are wrong, although it pains me to admit it.

'I'm going to need to improve on my French before I go. You can help me with that I'm sure!' Delilah had smiled but I knew that look. She had decided.

The conversation continued as the waiter cleared our plates with alarming efficiency. I tried to dissuade Delilah from pursuing French lessons, by telling her my French was more than a little rusty, as despite living there for some time, it was in fact almost forty years ago now.

'Oh pish.' She insisted. 'You've got the memory of an elephant Blake Hetherington and don't try telling me otherwise.'

The waiter had appeared once more, to take our

order for desert. They weren't normally quite so quick in The Snicket. It was one of the things I had liked about the place. They left you to enjoy your meal and didn't hassle you from one course to the next. Food should be taken seriously, not rushed. On this occasion, the service was a sign of the season. A week before Christmas and there was no rest for the waiter, or the eater as we were chivvied into ordering lemon posset, cheese and biscuits, a glass of amaretto, and a glass of port.

'Are you sure you don't mind looking after Bertie whilst I'm in Haiti?' Delilah had asked, for the third time that evening.

I had assured her there really was no problem and she promised to provide me with enough Bonio biscuits to keep Bertie from pining for her too much.

As the evening wore on, the noise from the table of office workers crescendoed, and it had reached a peak as our desserts arrived. I was starting to get the over-full feeling so often associated with Christmas. I sat up straight to make room for ample portions of fruited Wensleydale, Stilton and farmhouse matured Cheddar. I lifted my glass to my nose, closed my eyes and breathed in the aromas. Port is what Christmas was made for.

The waiter's uncouth shouting, from the bar, for Delilah interrupted my olfactory musings and as he approached the table I was all set to give him short shrift in regards to his indiscretion and lack of customer service skills, when a thought crossed my mind and stopped me.

Handing a pale blue Basildon Bond envelope to Delilah the waiter hurried off to harass another table for their dessert order. He had gone before Delilah could say 'Thank you.'

'How very odd' she said. Odd was about right.

That's what had stopped me in my tracks.

I placed my port glass back down on the table. This was most intriguing. Thirty maybe even twenty years ago it was not unusual to get a message delivered to your table but these days' people sent texts; in my opinion, an abomination of the written form. What was most unusual was that this was a sealed envelope. Not a piece of restaurant headed paper. This suggested that someone came into the restaurant to deliver the message to the waiter, as opposed to telephoning.

Delilah put down her spoon and opened the envelope. Her face visibly paled beneath her makeup, framed by her dark brown waves of hair, a tear appeared in the corner of her dark eyes and she was silent; a rarity for Miss Delibes.

'Is everything OK Delilah?' I'd fully expected the note to be a romantic gesture on the part of Rob. Perhaps inviting her to a tête-à-tête later that evening, I certainly wasn't expecting the fear, so evident, on Delilah's face.

She passed me the paper.

I've Always Found Marylands To Be Helpful

'It's Jay, it has to be!' Delilah said pushing her posset to one side.

'But he's in prison surely?' I said.

'Face it Blake, it wouldn't be the first time someone's escaped from prison would it?' Grabbing her glass, she knocked back the so far untouched amaretto, in one.

We sat in stunned silence. Neither of us continued to eat. The work party's conversation melted into white noise in the face of Delilah's poison pen letter.

'I think we had better leave.' I said.

Delilah didn't reply instead she sat staring at the sinister collage.

'We can go back to my house and ring Sergeant Claringdon. He'll know what to do.' I was trying to stay calm but the tremor in my voice gave me away. I was angry.

The idea of meeting our Texan friend again did not fill me with joy. Stalking Delilah took the biscuit. He was not going to get away with this. What was the world coming to when criminals could escape from prison and send threatening letters to innocent members of the public?

'But what if he's still out there Blake? I really think we should ring Rob now, don't you?' Delilah replied

'Nonsense. We are not giving Cartwright the satisfaction of a scene in my favourite, well, what was my favourite, restaurant. We're going to be British about this. I still have one good foot and I'll send him straight back to prison, with it firmly planted up his backside, let there be no doubt in your mind Delilah!'

Delilah laughed and a little of the colour returned to her cheeks. Well, I'd cheered her up a bit at least.

'OK,' she said. 'But let me ring Rob and get him to meet us at yours.'

Trying to get the waiter back, in order to pay the bill was harder than one might expect, given the speed with which he had served us earlier. It could have been that he sensed the tension at our table and dared not approach. Regardless, it was almost twenty minutes before we received the bill and paid. Yes, The Snicket was fast becoming my least favourite restaurant, conceivably doomed by their success.

Once safely back in Tuesbury, I put the kettle on and made us all a cup of blackberry tea with lavender honey. I'd made the tea with a recipe inherited from an old friend. Her notebook was bursting with little gems. I had no idea there were so many ways to make herbal teas. I always found the blackberry tea had a calming effect on one, and even Rob did not decline.

Tea in hand, we sat in my living room looking, once more, at the Basildon Bond.

'We'll have to analyse it of course.' Rob said, 'I've left a message for the governor at Wandsworth to confirm the location of Jay Cartwright.'

Delilah twisted the mug of tea in her hands, trying to control the tears at the mention of Cartwright's name.

'And we'll have to get you some police protection as well but I won't be able to arrange that until tomorrow.' Rob continued, 'It'll be someone from the Bestall force. You better stay with me tonight though.' He gave me a sideways look.

I knew he felt awkward about his relationship with Delilah. With neither of her parents playing a part in her life, Rob saw me as her surrogate father. I preferred to think of myself as a slightly eccentric uncle, and this avuncular gentleman was not unwise to the ways of the world. Gone were the days of dance cards and courting, with not even a touch of the knee before marriage. Youth was significantly more fickle these days.

'Thank you.' Delilah squeezed Rob's hand and gave a weak smile.

They made a quite a handsome pair sitting side by side on my Chesterfield. Both sat up straight, knees together, holding their mugs in cupped hands, on their laps. The Chesterfield was the sort of sofa that demanded respect.

'What about Bertie?' Delilah looked up at me, suddenly as she remembered her little dog. 'He must be wondering where I am!'

'I'll go and check on him,' I said

'I'd rather it was an officer, Mr Hetherington. We really don't know what this note means yet. It could be nothing more than a sick joke but I don't want you taking any risks. I'll send Alston round, he's on tonight.'

Despite Claringdon's insistence that I call him Rob, he continued to call me Mr Hetherington; a courtesy I allowed him to afford me. It was nice to find a young man with respect.

'Nonsense! Besides if one of your officers goes, Bertie won't recognise him and could bite him.'

I was trying to be helpful.

Delilah was indignant.

'Really Blake, how could you say such a thing? Bertie wouldn't bite a soul'.

I backed down. I knew when arguing with Delilah was fruitless. At least her indignation had taken her mind off the note for a moment.

'Do you really think it's a joke Rob?' Delilah asked.

'It's a possibility. The Gainsborough case was in all the papers. Perhaps it's some nut job seeking attention. I hate to say it, but it does happen.'

'That doesn't make me feel any better.' Delilah said.

Her shoulders hunched and legs crossed inward at the thought of her dilemma. She reminded me once more of her vulnerable side. Once more she was the girl who'd come to ask for my help at Hetherington's hats. The same compulsion to come to her aid, washed over me again.

'Biscuit?'

I offered a plate of chocolate chip cookies to the pair. I was still full from dinner and wasn't at all sure why I'd opened them, but lacking any other affirmative action I always found Maryland's to be very helpful.

They both shook their heads in unison, a little perplexed at my offer of frivolous fancies at such a time. I coughed apologetically and put the plate back on the table.

Thankfully, the bell saved me as Sergeant Claringdon's mobile rang. I'm pleased to say a normal traditional ringing tone, none of this jingling, jangling, tinny nonsense.

He answered with a very formal, 'Hello, Claringdon '. Almost as soon as he did, the telephone in the hallway started to ring.

I looked at the clock on the mantelpiece. It was almost midnight. There was no one who would be ringing at this time of night unless it was an emergency. I naturally got up to answer it fearing it could be my daughter.

'541 367.'

I always answered the phone with my number, something my daughter thought was very funny but it's always been my way.

'I know she's there.'

The reply was in a familiar Texan drawl. The phone was just offset from the doorway in to the living room. I could still see into the lounge. Rob was still on the phone and Delilah was listening in.

'Who is this?' I demanded.

Delilah was no longer listening to Rob. Alerted by my abruptness, she stood up from the sofa, spilling tea on the Axminster. The sergeant hung up his call and there was silence as we all looked at each other. The phone was still to my ear and as I received my response, I was trying not to think about the carpet.

'You know who it is Mr Hetherington. How about you let me speak to Miss Delilah, it'd be real nice, old man?'

It was Jay's voice. I was sure of it.

'She's not here.' I said

Registering the look on my face and realising this was no ordinary midnight phone call, Rob took two steps across the living room towards me.

'I know you're lying…' Jay started, but Rob, being a man of action, reached forward and took the phone from me.

'This is the police, who is this?' he barked down the receiver. But it was too late I could hear the click on the other end as Jay hung up.

Rob replaced the receiver in its cradle.

'Exactly what did they say Mr Hetherington?' he asked.

'I think it was Jay. It certainly sounded like him.' I said.

Delilah gave a little gasp and sat back down on the sofa, spilling yet more tea on the carpet. I went to take the mug from her, talking to Rob as I went.

'He wanted to speak to Delilah and he seemed to know she was here.' I said.

'Are you sure?' Rob replied

'Quite sure.'

Setting Delilah's mug down on the table, I then started soaking up the spilt tea with my hanky.

Delilah began to cry and I realised how insensitive I was being. Despite my desire to save the Axminster, I sat down next to her to try to offer some comfort.

'Everything will be alright Delilah, we can sort this out. Jay can't do anything to you.' I soothed. Having a daughter came in handy when dealing with emotional women, but I have to say I wasn't at all that used to dealing with an emotional Delilah.

Rob spoke; 'Damn straight he can't! That phone call I just had, confirms he's still in Wandsworth nick, where he should be! So who the hell was that!?'

Wherefore Art Thou Bonio

Several mugs of tea later and, unfortunately, more tears from Delilah, at one thirty in the morning it was decided, at that hour, there was little that could be done to resolve the situation. The tears were out of character and I blame fatigue and wine for the emotional version of Miss Delibes. Delilah went with Rob as arranged. She was, however, insistent that the next morning she should returned home to Bertie. Although, not without an unmarked police car stationed outside her house. It's amazing the service you receive when your amour is a detective.

I settled down to a restless night's sleep. I have never been very good at relaxing and situations such as these only served to increase the ticking of my brain.

At eleven the next morning the phone rang. It was Sergeant Claringdon informing me that Delilah was safely home and that Bertie had been predictably ecstatic to see her again. He also told me he was going to Wandsworth prison to speak to Jay Cartwright, in order to investigate further, the anonymous Texan caller. He expected to be there all day and would I mind dropping in on Delilah to check she was OK? I assured him that of course I would and that it had been my intention to do so.

I hung up the phone and looked down the hallway into the kitchen. The window has a splendid view of the one hundred foot garden attached to my bungalow. Whilst I had been on the phone, something had caught my eye.

At the bottom of the garden is a hawthorn bush. There's a gate in the hawthorn leading to the fields beyond; it's a little overgrown but still passable. I love hawthorn, it's good for the birds in the winter and so many of nature's wonders can make it their home. I have never had the heart to cut it back too hard.

There, standing in the gateway, silhouetted against a bright, cloudy, winter sky, was the unmistakable shape of a man. Six foot tall and of slight build; from this distance, he looked a lot like Jay Cartwright. Or at least what I can remember of him. It was over a year ago now that I had encountered the youngest of the Cartwright brothers and thankfully my acquaintance with him had been brief.

Claringdon had assured us that Jay was in Wandsworth prison and I had no reason to doubt him. He was, after all, in the know. More importantly this man was not wearing Jay's signature Breton. He was wearing a Stetson. Jay Cartwright was not a Stetson wearer. A Stetson required presence and character, neither of which Jay had.

If I hadn't known better I would have said it was the ghost of Hank Cartwright, but I have never believed in apparitions of any kind. There is always some explanation other than spectral manifestations of the soul.

Walking down the hall I got as far as the kitchen door, leading to the garden, before the figure made a run for it. Shouting out to him to stop, I ran down the garden path but I was too slow. The man was already halfway across the field by the time I reached the gate. Once more my old injury held me back. Rob had recommended an excellent physiotherapist who often worked with the police and although my foot was improving dramatically, it still wasn't back to fighting fit.

I gave up and retreated back indoors to ring Sergeant Claringdon and report the incident. There was no response. Perhaps he was out of signal, driving or already in Wandsworth talking to Jay. Whichever it was,

176

there was no point panicking. The man could have been anyone, although the coincidences were a little too much.

Lacking any other options, I decided to take the train to Delilah's earlier than I had planned. If this man had paid me a visit, perhaps he would be heading for her home too. I reassured myself that she would be fine. The officer outside would be doing their job. Grabbing my wax jacket and tweed cap I headed for the front door, collecting my wallet from the hallway table on the way.

I stopped at the florists on the High Street. I had decided Delilah might like some Gerberas better than the cookies I offered yesterday. The girl in the shop made a beautiful bouquet. She suggested some Gypsophila to complement the yellow Gerberas I had chosen. Yellow's such a happy colour. Wrapping them up she surrounded them in cellophane and tissue paper, all held together by a lovely orange ribbon, curled to perfection. I find the florist's art of arranging is almost as poetic as millinery.

As I left the shop, my phone started to buzz in my pocket. I'd almost forgotten it was there. I never used the mobile in the house, preferring the landline, so it just made sense to leave the mobile in my coat pocket. Unfortunately this meant that on occasion it ran out of battery. People usually had to leave a message.

This time, however, it did have some charge and I was there to answer it. A happy set of circumstances because it was Delilah. Her voice was high-pitched and slightly hysterical. This time there was no Sancerre to blame. I tried to calm her down and get her to make some kind of noise that my old ears were able to interpret.

'It's Bertie!'

'OK, just slow down a bit and try to tell me what's wrong.'

'I let him out into the garden to go for a wee and…' Delilah started sobbing again and I tried to steady my voice to hide my frustration. Hysterical women really were not my area of expertise.

'Is the officer outside still there? Should I speak to them?'

'No, no you can't do that. He says he's going to kill him….' She was wailing now.

'Who is? The officer?' I replied. I have a terrible habit of getting pedantic when I'm annoyed.

'No!' she shouted.

Maybe I should have controlled my tongue a little better. She was evidently very upset, but I was exasperated and now cold. I was still standing on the pavement outside the florist and it was starting to sleet. I'd forgotten my scarf and the wind was angling the precipitation straight down the back of my collar. I stepped back into the shelter of the florist porch.

'Ok Delilah, try and calm down. I can't help if I can't understand you.' I said.

I heard her stifle a few more sobs, sniff and finally collect her thoughts. When her voice returned to the phone she was not calm, but she now spoke in her more usual octave, and she was at least making sense.

'It's him again!'

'Carry on.' I encouraged. We were getting somewhere, although I was taking the involvement of the Texan as a given.

'I let Bertie out into the back garden and he was out there for about twenty minutes. I called him back in and he came no problem, but he had a little jacket on when he came back.' I could hear her voice starting to crack again.

'OK. What happened then?' I said, trying to keep her focused.

'Well it wasn't one of his coats I wouldn't buy a horrible bulky black thing like that. I bent down to unclip it but there was a note in his collar. Thank god I saw it because…' now she was sobbing again, '…because, oh poor Bertie, what am I going to do Blake?'

'What did the note say Delilah?' I had a very bad feeling about this. Who gave a Jack Russell a jacket as a gift, let alone sent it home with a note?

'It's too horrible Blake, too horrible.'

'Delilah, pull yourself together.' Sometimes a verbal slap is what is really needed and this time it did the trick.

'It's a bomb Blake!' then it all came out in a torrent of words. 'The note says it's a bomb. If Bertie goes back outside, or if the police come inside then he's going to detonate poor Bertie. It's horrible, I don't know what else to do. I can't get hold of Rob, his mobile's permanently going to answer phone and I don't dare speak to the policeman outside. If I ring the police I don't know what he'll do if they all turn up with guns and bomb squads. What if he sees me? He say he's watching me Blake, what am I going to do?'

I took a deep breath in. Delilah watched a little too many American police dramas for my liking but none the less, this was bad. Very, very bad.

'Right. I'm going to sort it out Delilah. I'm going to the police station and I'm going to talk to Alston, he'll know what to do.'

'OK' came a weak, crumpled reply. 'And Blake…'

'Yes?'

'I'm running out of Bonio.'

Abandoning the Gerberas

The police station in Tuesbury is about ten minutes walk from the High Street. I made it in five. I have no idea how my old bones carried me that quickly and by the time I got there my limp was definitely more pronounced.

Out of breath, hobbling, my jacket in disarray, and with a large bunch of yellow Gerberas, I asked, in stilted consonants, to see Detective Alston. The comedy of my arrival was not lost on the desk sergeant. Smirking, he left to find the detective and I collapsed on a polyester and foam-cushioned chair, which was screwed to the floor clearly designed not to encourage lingering.

What seemed like an age later, Detective Alston arrived. His amusement was also undisguised.

'Could I speak to you privately please Detective?' I smiled as sanely as possibly. It had now been almost fifteen minutes since Delilah had rung and I was painfully aware there was no knight in shining armour coming to her rescue just yet.

Alston frowned but, he relented with little fuss and showed me into an interview room just off the foyer. All the while the desk sergeant was clearly trying to suppress his urge to laugh at the montage I presented.

The door was barely shut before I started;

'Delilah's in trouble.'

'Okay Mr Hetherington, take a seat.'

'We haven't got time for any more sitting, Delilah's waiting for us to do something.' I was perhaps a little too impatient with a man who had none of the facts but I find bureaucracy intensely frustrating and where better to find it in full swing than a police station.

Alston on the other hand was embarrassingly reasonable.

'I'm very sorry Mr Hetherington but you haven't told me why Delilah's in trouble.'

I didn't want to wait any longer; I had no choice but to get straight to the point.

'Bertie's been strapped to a bomb.'

The detective's eyes widened.

'And who's Bertie?'

'Delilah's dog.'

'Ah. And where is the dog at the moment?'

'With Delilah in the house.'

'Well, then she needs to contact the police immediately.' Alston smiled, I'm still not sure he was taking me seriously at this point.

'Look detective, I am not a crackpot. Delilah is trapped in the house with a bomb dog and she can't leave or he'll detonate it. We have to do something!'

'Okay Mr Hetherington, perhaps we owe you a favour after all the help you gave us with the allotment case. I'm going to overlook the fact that none of this makes sense. We'll head over to Miss Delibes and perhaps you can give me the facts on the way there?'

'Thank you.' My shoulders relaxed and, I imagine, I may even have smiled.

'Of course you realise, if this is a wild goose chase, you'll be in all sorts of trouble. Wasting police time for a start.'

'I assure you constable this is not a wild goose chase. I wish it were.'

We left the station through a different door, avoiding the desk sergeant altogether. This was probably for the best as I was still clutching the gerberas, which were starting to lose their petals in all the excitement.

On the five-mile trip over to Deerton I brought Alston up-to-date with the situation. He had been unaware of the poison pen letter or last night's phone call, which went some way to explaining his previously relaxed and somewhat incredulous attitude in the interview room. As the information sunk in, his attitude changed and he became insistent on informing an armed response team, bomb squad, ambulance and fire service. Perhaps Delilah hadn't been exaggerating after all. This was just what she had been afraid of and I wasn't sure this was going to help her situation but Alston was adamant.

'We have our procedures Mr Hetherington and they are for the safety of all involved.'

He then had several conversations with various persons in authority and the upshot was the teams would meet a distance away from Delilah's house in the local convenience store car park. That would give the curtain-twitchers something to look at. Alston also assured me that Delilah would not be exposed to further danger. The armed response team would assemble out of sight and not even we would know where they were.

To my horror we drove past Delilah's house. It was unnervingly quiet. The officer outside was sat in an unmarked car, reading the paper. We too were not in a marked car and were thankfully not immediately recognisable as police. The officer didn't even look up from his paper as we drove past.

Alston finally parked around the corner from Delilah's. I protested. Surely we should go and see what we could do to help. Any delay should be avoided but Alston wasn't having any of it.

'Procedure Mr Hetherington, we must stick to procedure.'

Once parked up, Alston made a call to the officer outside the house. Some coded language was exchanged, that I do not pretend to understand suffice to say the police officer was to stay where he was, *'eyes on'*. Then he rang Delilah's house. I could hear how distressed she was from where I sat and I could hear Bertie barking in the background.

'Well?' I said as he hung up.

'We need to get a handle on this Mr Hetherington. I need you to stay here in the car whilst I go and talk to the Inspector.'

I said nothing only nodded as he left. I watched him in the rear view mirror, as he walked down the road several hundred metres and disappeared out of sight.

Frustrated, I threw the gerberas onto the back seat and pushed my hands into my pockets. My right hand fell on a plastic bag containing the familiar shape of dog biscuits. There was absolutely no way I was sitting there waiting for the police to formulate a plan. I had some of Bertie's favourites and Delilah needed my help.

Flying Dogs, Batman

I closed the car door as quietly as possible. I wasn't sure how far away Alston was and the street was deathly quiet. I had a moment of guilt at leaving the car unlocked but the detective had the keys.

I made my way quickly along the road to the T-junction. Delilah's was two houses down on the left. The street was empty apart from the original police officer in the car outside Delilah's house. I could see that the curtains of the houses opposite were closed and not a twitch stirred them.

I walked up the path to the front door without being stopped. I at least expected the police officer at the front of the house to try and prevent me from entering, but nothing happened and I daren't look back. I was also painfully aware that there might be guns pointed at my head. Alston did say they had deployed an armed response unit. Then again perhaps they were focussed on the wasteland at the back of the house; a far better place for a fugitive to stow himself.

I turned the handle of the door and found it unlocked. I eased it slowly open with just enough room to let myself in. How I failed to look suspicious to any of the police officers watching the house I still do not know, but I was aware that with dog biscuits in my pocket Bertie's nose would quickly alert him to my presence. I did not want him running out the door.

In a hoarse whisper I called to Delilah.

'Thank god you're here Blake' She said throwing her arms around me in a show of affection that was most unbecoming, but, given the circumstances, I allowed her this indiscretion and, patting her shoulder, released myself from her grip.

It was dark in the living room. Delilah hadn't opened the curtains, or perhaps she'd closed them, afraid of what may be outside. I did not ask.

Bertie was all over me like a rash. He'd identified the dog biscuit pocket and was setting about me as terriers do. I was thoroughly unnerved by the idea of a bomb-laden dog bouncing around my ankles and I gave up my booty quickly and without discussion. In fact, I threw them into the far corner of the living room as far away as possible. Delilah did not agree with the need to separate ourselves from *'poor Bertie'* and her bottom lip began to tremble once more.

'Has he rung you again?' Trying to distract her and stave off the tears.

'No' she replied

'Well, there are police everywhere so don't worry we'll get you out of this situation.'

'Everywhere? But he said…..'

'Don't worry, ' I interrupted. 'They know what they are doing.' I was not sure whom I was trying to convince. 'Now I had better ring Alston and see if I can help him from here.'

I picked up the phone and felt sick as I heard the ticking static of a dead line. My mobile had no reception; it never did here. Neither did Delilah's. It is one of the wonderful things about living in the country, unless of course, you find yourself, at the centre of a major incident.

'It's dead,' I said as I replaced the receiver. 'He must have cut the line.'

Delilah started to cry again. Bertie whimpered empathy from his corner but did not leave his prize. Biscuits devoured, he was now hunting for crumbs.

'Well, there's nothing else for it, I'd better make some tea.'

I walked into the kitchenette that adjoined the living room. I was on edge at the idea of communications being cut and my mind desperately searched for a solution. I picked up the kettle and took it to the sink to fill it. As I looked up at the window, I almost met my maker with the shock of seeing two figures peering in at me.

Recovering my composure, I opened the window, as requested by Sergeant Claringdon. At first I hadn't recognised the man with him. He had a thick beard, but on closer inspection I realised it was Jay Cartwright.

The last time I'd seen the youngest Cartwright, it had involved a lasting injury to my foot and I was not pleased to see him again.

'The phone was dead…is Delilah OK?' Claringdon asked immediately, through the open window.

'Yes', I said eyeing Cartwright. 'You shouldn't be here, he said no police, and why is he here?'

'That guy you're so keen to get your hands on, is my brother.' Cartwright answered for himself; his familiar voice producing an involuntary shudder on my part. 'I hear he's threatened my Delilah.'

Claringdon was very calm given the circumstances. I, on the other hand, wanted to punch Jay, square in the face and not for the first time. I resisted. It wasn't going to help anyone.

'Shut up Cartwright,' Claringdon jerked the cuffs that held the two of them together. 'We'll sort this out Mr Hetherington. Is Bertie still in there?'

Bertie had been silent for quite some time now, save for the munching of biscuits. Now, at the sound of Claringdon's voice and the mention of his name, he came bounding into the kitchen followed by Delilah who was shouting for someone to stop him.

There was no way she could catch the agile terrier as he leapt onto the draining board. A blur of russet brown and white fur, a flash of that oh so familiar doggy smell and Bertie was out of the window. Sergeant Claringdon instinctively ducked to avoid a full frontal assault and Bertie was off across the wasteland. In his little doggy mind, the presence of Claringdon meant play time.

I didn't really think about what to do next, it was simply instinct. Bertie had left the building; his very life was in danger. After all, he was one of us. I turned from the window, took two steps to the back door, opened it and started running after him.

I'd almost caught up with him when the shooting started. This time I was grateful for instinct as I threw myself at the ground, I am ashamed to say with my eyes tightly shut. As if my situation was not undignified enough, Bertie thought better of his escape and returned to lick my face.

The shooting stopped as abruptly as it started and silence fell once more. I was left in the middle of the wasteland with a small dog and, I thought, a bomb but as I looked up, I realised he was sans jacket.

That meant only one thing. Not wanting to get up for fear of being shot, but concerned for the welfare of my comrades in the house, I turned on my side to take in the scene behind me. I looked back just in time to see Sergeant Claringdon disappearing through the kitchen window. Why the window I still have no idea, when there was a perfectly good door, three steps around the corner. Perhaps windows offer less impedance to ones trajectory. As the sergeant disappeared, Jay Cartwright started to run. He had been uncuffed so Claringdon could complete his reverse defenestration.

I was faced with a decision. Accost Jay Cartwright for a second time in my life, or grab Bertie and see if I could do something to save Delilah and Rob. Neither of these options were likely to be particularly good for my health.

I chose the latter, grabbed the plucky Jack Russell and started to move towards the house in half commando crawl. As I progressed, a small black item was thrown from the kitchen window and landed in front of me. I knew what it was. The only option left to me now was to run.

But I was running through treacle, my legs were heavy with cramp from kneeling and would not move fast enough, I just prayed I would be far enough away before the inevitable.

I hit the ground again, covering Bertie and hoping I did not do him any lasting damage. I landed heavily on my right shoulder, as I tried to direct my weight away from the little dog. Behind us, the deafening sound of an explosion ripped through the air.

Crumbs

Thankfully, there had only been enough explosives in the jacket to blow up a dog but that did not mean I escaped without injury. My collarbone throbbed.

Behind me, a little remote vehicle approached the scorched earth of the detonated bomb and, as a gentleman never sheds a tear in public, I started to laugh.

I looked up to see Rob and Delilah, at the kitchen window, staring at the dishevelled hysterical OAP. Bertie had wriggled free and was scampering back across the field to Delilah. I was looking forward to the explanation for this one but I was going to have to wait. As I stood up, I realised they weren't looking at me.

Across the other side of the wilderness that backed onto Delilah's house two figures were making their way towards us. They appeared to be handcuffed together. The next minute, shouts emanating from the bushes had them both lying flat on the ground as armed police surrounded them.

Once the ambulance in attendance had treated our injuries, we returned to the station for, what I know from past experience is, terrible coffee and an explanation from Sergeant Claringdon.

The loss of a father, a messy divorce and a patricidal brother had all been too much for Owen John Cartwright. John, as the family called him, had blamed Delilah for this and had been bent on revenge. Any information he needed he had gleaned from Jay who had simply been pleased that one member of his family was actually visiting him in prison.

Jay thought that John was going to help him get Delilah back; little did he know. When Jay found out from Sergeant Claringdon what was going on he immediately knew who it was and came over all community spirited. He knew it had to be his brother and he knew he wasn't bluffing. John had previous military experience and the knowledge to rig a bomb.

Claringdon had become anxious when the lines were cut and decided to see for himself what was going on in the house. He hadn't banked on Bertie being quite so pleased to see him. Unable to follow me with a cuffed prisoner and then having to duck for cover when the shooting started, the detective had looked on in horror as I bounded after Bertie. I had not been aware at the time that the shooting had in fact been at me. The police snipers had thought I was something to do with the hostage situation. Claringdon had quickly radioed them to stop. Even so an angel must have been watching over me for such trained marksmen to miss me entirely.

Once my safety was secured, Claringdon could see that Bertie had lost his deadly jacket. Realising the little scamp had chewed though the strap, Claringdon looked through the window and saw that the bomb now lay on the kitchenette floor. He released Jay in order to perform his heroic leap.

It was then that Jay made a run for it, it transpires, to reason with his brother, aware that he may remotely detonate the device as previously threatened. A fight had ensued and the explosion occurred in the struggle, mercifully with no injury to those involved in the incident. Jay eventually got the upper hand, handcuffed himself to his brother and returned to the house. Perhaps there was a shred of decency in in the man after all. Maybe this is what Delilah had seen in him.

It was dark by the time I left the police station. Exhausted and in pain, I had instructions to attend A & E for a suspected fractured collarbone. I refused to be driven there by a police officer. In my opinion it would have been an unnecessary use of resources. The ambulance on scene had given me a sling; all I needed now was to rest. The pain was nothing that I couldn't banish with some of the painkillers I had left over from last year's foot injury. I'd known keeping them would come in handy again at some point. I'd visit the hospital in the morning before travelling to Devon.

Delilah was going to stay with Rob for a few nights, Bertie too, of course. He had recovered from his brush with death much quicker than any of us. If he hadn't chewed that jacket off in his attempts to retrieve the biscuit crumbs caught under it, he might now be part of Delilah's wallpaper.

I stood on the pavement outside the station waiting for my taxi. It was a cold, dark December evening, but a peaceful one. The luminous Christmas star hanging from the lamppost opposite squeaked in the breeze and the smell of open fires hung in the air. I was glad today was over. The sound of the taxi pulling up was dulled by the snow-laden sky and, as I got into the car, the clouds started to release their fat white flakes.

'Looks like it'll be a white Christmas' the taxi driver said

'Indeed,' I replied resting my head back on the headrest and closing my eyes. I hoped it wouldn't snow too much and disrupt the trains to Devon. I was very much looking forward to being fussed over by my daughter; although how I was going to explain away my latest injury I had no idea. How could I expect her to believe I had received it rescuing a Jack Russell from a delusional bomber? No, I had better just tell her I fell off a ladder whilst clearing out the guttering. Contented I settled into the back seat, hypnotised by the soporific tones of the taxi driver discussing the weather. I'd soon be home for Christmas.

Thank you for reading 'The Blake Hetherington Mysteries.' If you've enjoyed reading, then further information, on existing and future publications by D S Nelson, is available at **www.dsnelson.co.uk**

To sign up for D S Nelson's newsletter, for news on upcoming publications, events and offers, please visit the website or use the QR code below.

You can follow D S Nelson via:

Twitter:

@WriterDSNelson

Facebook:

www.facebook.com/WriterDSNelson

Wordpress:

www.hatpaintladdersandwonkypooh.wordpress.com